WRAPPED UP IN LOVE

C. A. KRAUSE

This book is a work of fiction. Names, characters, places, or incidents either are products of the author's imagination or are used fictitiously. Any resemblance to actual events or locales or persons, living or dead, is entirely coincidental.

Copyright © 2022 C.A. Krause

Ebook ISBN: 978-1-990703-07-2

Paperback ISBN: 978-1-990703-08-9

All rights reserved, including the right to reproduce this book or portions thereof in any form whatsoever.

Cover by GetCovers

TO MY READERS

This book is a work of fiction and the events in it take place much quicker than they tend to in real life. Remember, trust needs time and should never be rushed. I do not recommend readers attempt any of the practices found in this book based on my descriptions. Again, this is a work of fiction and is only intended for my readers' entertainment, not for educational purposes.

That being said, I very much hope you enjoy the story and characters.

I appreciate every one of you!

C.A.

Chapter One

Tamara

"What are you doing on Christmas Day, then?"

Tamara considered making up something to avoid her friend's pity, but decided against it.

"I'll probably stay home, drink hot chocolate, eat too much junk, and binge watch Christmas movies."

Casey leaned back against the couch, looking worried, and Tamara felt the love of her friend in that expression.

"You could come spend the day with us, you know?"

The cream colors of the décor in Casey's living room, where they were sitting, matched her friend's calm personality. Unlike the bright pillows, curtains, and rugs in her own house.

She shook her head. "Thank you, but no." There was no way she wanted to intrude on Casey's and Andrew's first Christmas as a married couple. Spending the holidays alone really wasn't a big deal to her, anyway.

Especially this year.

Sitting on the plush beige carpet in her friend's house was a reminder of what she was missing out on if she only did scenes at the club. Not being allowed to sit on the furniture was one of the rules Andrew had for his wife when Tamara came over to visit. While Tamara had made a few jokes about it in the beginning, she secretly loved it each time she visited. It was a sweet way in which Andrew included Tamara in their dynamic and she knew it for what it was: Andrew's way of showing he welcomed her into their home and family.

As was his occasional meddling in her life. *Consider me your big brother*, he'd told her at his and Casey's wedding reception.

"I've actually found the perfect way to treat myself this year."

"Oh, yeah?" Casey was definitely intrigued.

"Did you read the club newsletter last week?" Casey and Andrew were members of Club B as well, so they should have received the monthly email Jessica sent out.

"No, it's still sitting in my inbox. Is Jessica hosting a Christmas party?"

Tamara grinned. "Not exactly. There will be a Christmas themed auction to benefit the local women's shelter. And I've signed up."

Casey's eyes grew wider. "What kind of auction?" Despite her question, her excited expression told Tamara she had already guessed the answer.

"The newsletter said that anyone who is free over the Christmas holiday can sign up to be auctioned off. Even dominants if they want to, though I bet it'll be a bunch of us subbies doing it."

"Shut up!" Casey exclaimed. "That's such a cool idea."

"I know, right? I bet Mistress Vivienne is organizing it, so it's bound to be really cool."

Casey nodded. Mistress Vivienne was a good friend of the club owner, and, as an event planner, usually organized all the bigger events held by Club B.

"So you already signed up? What will you have to do?"

Tamara shook her head. "I guess it depends on who wins me." A giggle escaped her at the strange sentence and Casey joined in. "I had to fill out a new limits list for the event and specify which days I'd be available for whoever wins me. Some people get auctioned off for just a scene, while others do a full day, or even more."

Casey raised her left eyebrow, a move Tamara could never copy. Sadly, her own eyebrows preferred to be raised together, a real bummer when trying to prod doms with sassy facial expressions.

"Well, don't make me ask all the questions! What did you sign up for?"

Feeling the telltale prickle of a blush on her cheeks, she admitted, "I must have had too many glasses of wine when I filled out the form. I said I'd do a full three days."

Casey's eyes went round. "Are you serious? You've never done full-time subbing before."

"Well, I wouldn't be a full-time slave or service sub during that time or anything. It's more that whoever wins me has access to me whenever he wants during that time." She was pretty sure her face grew even redder at her admission, even though she knew Casey would be the last person on earth to judge her. Maybe even beyond that, if those alien romances had some truth to them and there was extraterrestrial life.

If Casey and she ever ended up on a different planet somewhere, they'd still be the best of friends. No hot, green aliens would ever come between them. Of course, Andrew would come and get his wife before any alien ever laid a hand or tentacle on her, anyway.

"Hot damn, girlfriend. You weren't kidding when you said you'd treat yourself." At that, they both broke into fits of hysterics until Andrew walked into the room, giving them a scrutinizing expression.

"What are you two up to?" he asked as he walked over, taking Casey's ponytail in his hand and tugging on it softly.

Casey tilted her head back to smile at her Master. "Tamara is getting herself a dom for Christmas."

At Andrew's amused expression, the two of them started laughing again.

"I take it you signed up for Jessica's auction?" he asked when they'd stopped to catch their breath.

"You knew about it?" Casey asked, clearly affronted her dom hadn't shared the news with her.

"Of course I did. Unlike someone else in this house, I actually read my emails."

While Casey pouted, Tamara looked up at Andrew. "I did."

He nodded. "I think that's an excellent idea."

This time, neither Casey nor Tamara laughed, instead they both narrowed their eyes at Andrew.

"What do you mean by that?" his wife asked him suspiciously.

Andrew laughed. "Nothing more than what I said. I think it's great Tamara is putting herself out there."

His serious tone reminded Tamara of what he'd told her recently. Andrew wasn't just her best friend's husband, but also her friend and honorary big brother, so when he'd pulled her aside to ask why she hadn't tried scening with new people or pushing her limits lately, she hadn't been able to stop thinking about it. Before, she hadn't even realized that she was doing it, sticking to familiar partners and scenes, but once Andrew had pointed it out, she'd realized that she had fallen into a pattern.

It wasn't really a surprise.

She might be an adventurous person at heart, but she also liked anything that gave her life stability. Case in point, she still lived in the same tiny apartment she'd rented when she first started college, even though she could easily afford something nicer now, despite her underpaid position as a social worker. Instead, she stayed there. It was her home and that meant something to her, given that she'd grown up without a place to call her own.

"What day is the auction?" Casey asked suddenly. "I'd like to come and watch."

"I was planning for us to go," Andrew said. "It's on the second Saturday in December."

"That's only two weeks away," Casey exclaimed. "Do you have something to wear yet?"

Tamara grinned at her best friend. "Nope. I was thinking we are overdue for a shopping trip."

Casey beamed, and Andrew grinned. "Nice."

With a kiss on Tamara's head, Andrew turned and walked out of the room, leaving them to plan. Casey's husband was a sucker for role playing, so he hardly ever objected to Casey going out and buying new clothes.

Tamara sighed. What she wouldn't give for a relationship like that.

Two weeks later, the club looked beautiful. There were Christmas trees, garlands, wreaths, and stars. Everything a person needed to get into the Christmas spirit. Not that she wasn't already well into the spirit. Reds, greens, and gold decorated her tiny apartment, and she'd visited the Christmas market just yesterday.

There wasn't a holiday she adored more than Christmas, even if she always celebrated it alone.

Instead of the usual music, Christmas carols played, changing the entire atmosphere of the club from dungeon to kinky north pole. It was epic. There was even a little hot chocolate station at the bar with marshmallows, whipped cream, and red and green sprinkles.

This was as good as it got. Even the scent of the citrusy cleaner that always reminded her of orgasms and sex only added to her good mood. The only thing that was making her a little uneasy was the stage that was set up where usually the dance floor was. She was definitely getting some last-minute jitters. Not about the auction itself, of course. She might have fallen into a pattern with her behavior, but a coward she was not.

Getting auctioned off? Not a problem. But being up on a stage? A little nerve-wrecking. Especially since these weren't just any men bidding. They were doms, and if anyone asked her, they were a species all of their own, and they'd definitely fall into the predator category.

But, now that she'd identified her complacency problem, she was full-steam ahead in fixing it. When you had only yourself to rely on from a young age, you learned to do what needed to be done to ensure your own happiness and future.

So here she was, getting herself a Christmas present.

She pulled down the white lace of her skirt. Jessica had emailed saying they should all wear some sort of

Christmas costume to make the auction even more fun, so Casey and she had gone out and had a blast finding the perfect outfits.

An angel costume seemed to be an appropriately amusing choice for a BDSM club.

As she headed to the assigned meeting place, one of the theme rooms, she saw others who'd donned costumes and were walking in the same direction. When she spotted Presley, she waved, and he came over to fall into step next to her.

"You look gorgeous," he said, grinning at her outfit. "Positively angelic."

She laughed at his bad joke. "Looking good yourself."

He was wearing a rather naughty elf costume that would make Santa blush a beet red.

"Right?" Presley twirled so she could admire his costume from all sides.

She gave him a thumbs up. "Are you in the auction?"

Presley beamed, showing none of her last-minute jitters. "Yup. I'm giving myself away for a steaming hot scene with any Master who thinks he can handle a real Christmas treat."

Tamara grinned. "I can beat that. I'm giving away three days."

Presley's eyes widened. "For real?"

"Yeah, I didn't have any other plans, so I figured, why not?"

Sympathy showed in Presley's eyes, and Tamara regretted her words. There was nothing worse than bringing down a perfectly cheerful mood, and there was no reason to reveal anything about her less than brag-worthy holiday plans.

Except, if things went well today, she might just get the most exciting Christmas holiday she'd had in years. Or ever, really.

They reached the Daddy/Mummy Dom room and walked in. There were already a good number of people in the room, maybe fifteen, though it was difficult to count in the slightly cramped space.

Tamara had never played in here, since she'd never fancied herself a baby girl, but she had to admit the set-up was pretty amazing. The walls were all pink, and a four-poster bed with princess curtains all around dominated the room. There were stuffed animals on shelves along the walls, and even the sex toys on display in a glass cabinet were baby blue and pink.

"Tamara and Presley, it's good seeing you two. Come over here please, so I can sign you in," Jessica called from where she sat on the bed, a sheet of paper next to her on the bedside table.

After they'd signed in, they joined the other submissives, everyone happily showing off their costumes, until the door opened and everyone grew quiet, except for Jessica, who chuckled.

Master Dominic walked in wearing a Santa-suit. Without a shirt. His red and white jacked gaped open, exposing his toned chest, making it very hard not to stare at least a little.

"Well, fuck me," Presley muttered next to her. "If I'd known I could bid on a scene with Master Dominic, I wouldn't have signed up myself."

Tamara laughed. "You should ask Jessica if you can still do it. I don't see why you shouldn't be able to bid when it's not your turn in the auction."

Presley's eyes brightened. "That's an excellent idea."

When the excitement of everyone realizing that one of the Masters had actually signed up to be auctioned off had passed, Jessica got up and addressed the group.

"Thank you all for taking part in the auction and donating your time to raise some money for a good cause. I won't bore you with a speech now, since I'll be doing that later on stage, so I'll hand it over to Mistress Vivienne, who will give you instructions on what you need to do during the auction."

The tall domme that had walked in sometime after Master Dominic stepped in front of the group wearing fuck-me heels that gave Tamara acrophobia just looking at them. "Hello everyone." She surveyed the group, giving them all a stern assessment. "Please listen carefully to my instructions. I don't wish to repeat them. I'll have you all line up on stage so everyone can see who's up for auction. The audience has received flyers with the information you submitted about limits, availability, and your time offer. When your name gets called, you'll step up next to me and I will start the bidding process. If you like, you can pose for the audience, but you can also just stand or kneel. Whatever you feel most comfortable with."

"Can we bid on each other?" Presley asked, throwing a flirtatious look in Master Dominic's direction, who acknowledged it with an appreciative grin.

Mistress Vivienne smiled, the expression transforming her face to look a little less like she might pull out a whip at any moment. "Certainly. Anyone who wants to join in the bidding is welcome to do so. Of course, you can't bid on yourselves, but everyone else is fair game as long as you meet the bidding requirements in the flyer."

When signing up, the form allowed them to specify what kind of partner they were looking for. Tamara had filled out male and dominant, since she was heterosexual and submissive. Given that she'd seen Master Dominic play with male subs in the past and figured he'd have included as much on the flyer, she gave Presley a thumbs up. Looked like he'd be bidding on his own Christmas present tonight.

"All right everyone, it's time to make some money for a good cause and have some fun doing it!" Mistress Vivienne announced. "Everyone, please follow me."

Tamara got in line and forced herself to take a few deep breaths. It was time to get up on a stage and cross her fingers that someone good would bid for her so she wouldn't spend another Christmas holiday gorging way too many Christmas cookies.

She still wanted some cookies of course, but she wouldn't mind feasting on something else, too.

Chapter Two

Ken

Ken's phone vibrated in his pocket. Checking to see that his last counseling client for the day had left the office, he pulled it out to read the message.

Thought you'd be interested.

Intriguing, though surprising since the message came from Andrew, a fellow Club B dominant who was more of an acquaintance than someone who regularly texted him. Attached was a link to the members only area of the Club B website. Curious, Ken headed to his desk and logged into the website before opening the page Andrew had sent him.

A Christmas Auction at Club B. Great, just what he wanted. Not.

He picked up his phone again.

Why?

Andrew's response was immediate, as if he'd expected Ken's answer.

Casey's friend Tamara signed up. Noticed you checking her out. Nice way to do some good over the holidays...

Turning his attention back to the desktop, Ken scanned the list of names. There it was.

Tamara Loonsey.

Admittedly he had been checking her out a few times and obviously he hadn't been very subtle about it. Not that there was any reason to be when both of them were playing in a public kink club. Watching others play was half of the fun and the little sprite seemed well at ease and usually full of energy.

He wasn't shy about approaching women he wanted to play with, but the little blonde was hard to catch. She seemed to stick to the same pre-arranged play partners and disappeared from the club right after. Eventually, he would have found the time to make a pass anyway, but this was the perfect opening.

If only it wasn't a damned Christmas party.

Still, after yet another session with a patient who had to work through trauma surrounding this merry season he might as well follow his own advice and seek out something positive in order to attract better thoughts. He'd been playing the avoidance game for a long time, and the increased drain he'd been experiencing this year was starting to take a toll on him.

This auction might not be a miracle cure, but the thoughts that came to mind when picturing Tamara were definitely of the positive variety

Yes, he might as well give it a try.

His conviction that coming to Club B today was a good idea was quickly dwindling.

Whoever the fuck thought it was a good idea to put Christmas stars on top of a St. Andrew's Cross was a lunatic. This was a BDSM club, not the freaking North Pole. Except it looked like everyone else was embracing the Christmas spirit.

Ken sighed.

This was near torture, but then again, he was happy to donate to a worthy cause, like the women's shelter that would receive the proceeds from the auction. If it allowed him to get a foot in the door with the elusive little blond he'd been watching, even better.

But that didn't mean he had to enjoy walking through Christmas hell.

He usually did everything he could to avoid being exposed to the commercialized holiday that put everyone else in a frenzy.

"You look mighty cheerful," his cousin greeted him with a smirk.

"Screw you." He embraced Johnathan in a quick side hug.

"I wasn't sure you'd actually show."

"I told you I was coming."

"You did, but then there's Christmas trees and garlands around, so it wasn't a sure bet."

Ken scoffed, refusing to take the bait.

"What's made you so determined to brave the festivities?" Johnathan's gaze took on that *I'm a perceptive mother-fucker* look he used on submissives when he tried to figure something out. It only barely managed to cover up the concern in his cousin's tone.

Johnathan might be a well-liked and powerful dominant, but his antics weren't going to work on Ken.

"I came for the auction." Why else would he be here?

"Plan on bidding on one of the subbies?" Now Johnathan winked, apparently having accepted his reason.

"Sure am."

"Which one? Someone specific?" Obviously intrigued now, Johnathan's never ending cheer was about as different from Ken's serious personality as they came, but despite their differences, he and Johnathan were as close as brothers.

Ken nodded towards the stage. "Yep. Tamara. She's the one wearing the angel dress."

All the subbies on stage had donned costumes that ranged from sexy Mrs. Clause to sexy Christmas Elf, to sexy Gingerbread Man. Really, there was a somewhat disconcerting lack of range despite the usually so creative submissives of the club.

They were all kneeling in a neat row, supervised by Master Jeffrey. On one side of the stage, Master Dominic was standing and waiting, clearly amused by the entire event.

Ken chuckled as he watched Jeffrey correct a few of the subs on their positions. "Looks like none of the little subbies are going to dance out of line today." Jeffrey was known as one of the most skilled sadists of the club, though since he'd collared a newbie masochist his play had tamed a bit. Based on the scenes Ken had witnessed them do, he guessed it was a temporary measure while Jeffrey was easing his partner into the more intense stuff.

"That's for sure." His cousin agreed, looking amused. "None of them would dare dance out of line while Jeffrey is in charge. Jessica was smart to talk him into volunteering for this."

WRAPPED UP IN LOVE

Before Johnathan could further grill him on his plans for the evening, Mistress Vivienne stepped onto the stage and everyone fell quiet. The woman knew how to draw attention.

"Good evening everyone and happy holidays!"

Cheers rose from all around the large room.

"Tonight we are hosting the first ever Club B charity auction."

Again, everyone clapped and Vivienne had to wait a few moments before she could continue.

"You should all have received an info sheet from John at the entrance. If you haven't received one, you can still get one from the bar. Bidding will start at the listed price. With that being said, let's start the fun!"

Amused, Ken watched as one after another the Club B submissives were being auctioned off. With bids starting between twenty and fifty dollars and final bids going up to two hundred bucks, the club members were ensuring a sizable contribution would go to the women's shelter.

After she had auctioned the first five submissives off, Vivienne grinned at the crowd as if she were imitating the Cheshire cat. "Next up, we have a particular treat. The only Master brave enough to do so, Master Dominic agreed to be auctioned off to one very lucky submissive tonight. This might be your only chance to ever win a Master of Club B, so bidding will start at one hundred dollars. We welcome bids from submissives of all genders and identities, and Master Dominic has told me he's already come up with a rather nice role playing scene he wants to do with whomever wins him tonight."

Various hands shot into the air and Vivienne conducted the auction as if she worked for a large auction house, the price driving higher and higher. Even two of the submissives on stage started bidding, and it was damn near impossible for Ken not to be amused by the Master who was standing on stage, happily drawing the attention of a large group of the club's submissives. Even if he was wearing a Santa suit.

"Damn, now I wish I had signed up," Johnathan said, laughing.

Ken chuckled. "You'd have enjoyed it, no doubt."

"The highest bid is 400 dollars. Do I hear anyone say 450?"

"Going once, going twice, sold. Master Dominic will top Presley in a steamy Christmas role-play."

The crowd broke out into cheers. Ken tuned them out while the next couple of submissives were being auctioned off, sipping his drink. His attention only returned to the stage when Mistress Vivienne called Tamara's name.

"And now we have a very special offer. Tamara is donating a full three days to a male dominant who is looking for some Christmas fun. You heard that right. Three days with this lovely submissive. While she looks like an angel, her interests include bondage and impact play. She enjoys pain in scenes, but does not consider herself a masochist. And, if you aren't tempted yet, you should know that she wouldn't mind licking something other than icicles over the holidays."

Tamara's skin was turning a rosy pink, visible even this far from where she stood. It was a safe bet that every single unattached dom in this place was wondering if her skin took that same beautiful shade after a spanking. Not only that, but she had offered not just a scene, but three full days.

She didn't do things half-way, it seemed. The thought was appealing, especially when combined with her declared interest in treating herself and the dom who won her to some delicious licking action.

Fuck.

This wasn't going to be a bid he'd get to win easily, and while he made good money as a psychologist, he had recently purchased a home. Combined with the budget he'd set aside to spoil his nieces for Christmas, that meant he was going to have to stick strictly to the $500 he was planning on donating tonight.

Master Dominic had only offered one scene, and he'd sold at 450 dollars.

Besides the fact that he hadn't known what Tamara's offer tonight would be, he had definitely miscalculated the amount the Club B crowd was willing to spend, which was naïve, given that he knew that the exclusive club's membership alone meant that most members had a fair amount of disposable income. He probably would have known better if he'd been around more, but he'd missed more than a couple weeks because he'd stayed at the office late, talking to patients who found this time of year equally as difficult as he did.

Well, he'd just have to wait and see.

"Our opening ask is $100 dollars for three days with lovely Tamara. Do I hear $100?"

Ken saw several doms raising their ridiculous Christmas-tree shaped bidding cards. He didn't bother raising his own. Only when the price reached 450 dollars and Mistress Vivienne asked for more bids, did Ken raise his bidding card, knowing he wouldn't win.

Johnathan

After watching his cousin's expression grow frustrated, Johnathan figured he was just about at the limit of what he had put aside for this little game. And it looked like Ken wasn't happy about being outbid.

He let his eyes flick back to the young submissive his cousin had picked out as an object of his desire. She was pretty enough, although less curvy than he usually preferred his women. She wasn't someone he'd paid particular attention to in the club before, but now that his attention was on her, he realized that, at a second glance, she was intriguing. The way Tamara's cheeks had flushed when Vivienne introduced her had certainly drawn more than a few appreciative looks.

Standing next to Mistress Vivienne, looking slightly wide-eyed, her soft blonde waves fell over her shoulders, and it almost looked like her hair sparkled. He wondered if she'd used some sort of product to make it look that way, or if her hair just naturally had that shine to it. It definitely helped her look like the angel she'd dressed up as.

She had a small, slightly pointy nose, giving her a pixie-like look. The thought made him chuckle. His nieces loved books about fairies and pixies and, as they were only six and four, all of their books still came with illustrations, meaning he'd been reading a lot of picture books lately. Tamara looked like she could have stepped right out of any one of those pages.

The angel costume worked too. She definitely had that innocent look about her. And he wondered if that was what attracted his cousin.

WRAPPED UP IN LOVE

It was curious that Ken was here today. Usually it was a useless effort to motivate him to attend any sort of Christmas event, even family ones. And getting Ken a present? Forget it. It was like trying to cheer up the Grinch himself.

Well, it looked like this year there was something his cousin wanted for Christmas, so he might as well indulge the guy. Maybe it would loosen him up enough to actually attend their grandmother's dinner. That would be a win no-one in the family could deny, even if they wouldn't have a clue how Johnathan had managed it.

He leaned over to speak into his cousin's ear. Better to make his offer privately. "I'll tell you what, let's combine funds."

Suspicion showed in Ken's eyes when he turned to look at him. "Why would you want to do that?"

Suggesting it was a Christmas present would be a sure way to receive a rejection. Unfortunately, his cousin was too smart to be outplayed, so some careful negotiations were in order. "As a bribe to come to granny's Christmas dinner."

Ken stared at him for a moment before shaking his head slowly. "No."

Johnathan rolled his eyes. "Fine. Then how about because I'm in the mood to share?"

That got his cousin's interest. They'd topped together a few times in the past, and it had been fun. Actually, it had been some of the best scenes he'd ever done, but co-topping had been challenging to arrange, so it had been a while since they'd indulged in that particular fun.

"You want to share Tamara?"

Johnathan looked back at the stage. Her eyes were on them, watching with interest. Not that she could hear what they were saying. "Sure, I've always wanted to taste an angel."

Grinning, Ken nodded. "Let's do it. How much are you thinking?"

"I was planning on two-fifty, but let's see how the bidding goes."

Again, his cousin nodded, looking over at Mistress Vivienne, who was asking for the next bid.

Ken raised his stake, calling out a higher bid now that Johnathan had injected some extra cash into his bidding fund. Almost immediately, someone else outbid them. Ken's brows furrowed, while Tamara stood wide eyed on stage, looking between Ken and the other bidder.

Johnathan tried to see who it was, but he couldn't get a line of sight. It didn't really matter.

Ken raised his stake. Again, they were outbid.

It was turning into a rather displeasing pattern.

"The next bid will be seven-fifty. That's our cap." Ken wasn't one to break rules he'd set for himself.

It was the responsible thing to do, but Johnathan wasn't about to let this opportunity slip through his fingers. "Two more bids. I have it covered. It's for a good cause, after all."

Ken raised his eyebrows at him. Usually his cousin would have looked disapproving, but this time he obviously couldn't get himself to say anything. He must really want to win this bid.

"Do it." Johnathan injected his commanding dom tone into the words, making Ken smile slightly. They both knew there wasn't a submissive bone in Ken's body, but he did as Johnathan had suggested and raised his little Christmas tree cut out.

How ironic. The Grinch was in Christmas mode now.

One bid later, they'd won themselves a little submissive for Christmas, and Johnathan found himself oddly elated at the idea that he too would get a Christmas treat this year.

On stage, the little angel looked speechless at the amount Ken had just spent. With a little grin, Johnathan pictured some other creative ways to make the innocent-looking subbie speechless. Yes, this would be a very fun holiday.

Chapter Three

Tamara

"Going once, going twice, sold for 900 dollars! This little angel goes to Master Ken."

The submissive next to Tamara turned her head. "Wow, that was exciting. That's by far the highest bid tonight."

There were no words to describe the adrenaline pumping through her right now. A nervous giggle escaped her. "Right?"

She couldn't quite get over the fact that the bids had gone so high. Part of her was thrilled that her participation in the auction would mean a sizable donation to the women's shelter, but the other half was trembling at the prospect of meeting Master Ken. She'd seen him around the club, but they'd never even spoken. He was one of those really intimidating people who did more watching than mingling, and she usually had little time to hang out since she always carpooled with Casey and Andrew. It was one of her safety measures. Which meant that she didn't know what to expect other than he had an excellent reputation as a dom.

WRAPPED UP IN LOVE

What would a Master who was willing to spend this much money to spend time with her have planned for their time together?

Once the auction ended, the nervous tingle inside her grew to epic proportions. Everyone clapped and Mistress Vivienne, who had organized the event, directed them all to follow her down to the dungeon.

Jessica had limited the festivities to the upstairs for today. Downstairs, they had set up a place for them to meet the Masters who had won their bids. There would be negotiations, supervised by some of the club monitors or senior members. It was another precaution Jessica had put in place to make sure that everything would abide by the safe, sane, and consensual rules of the BDSM community. It was something Tamara appreciated about the club and the main reason she was willing to put away some of her less than impressive monthly salary for the membership fees.

At other times, members might engage in more risk-aware kink, but for this auction, Jessica had strictly limited play to safe, sane, and consensual, which made sense to keep things light and was much more up Tamara's alley, anyway.

She followed the others down the stairs, working hard not to swivel her head and search for Master Ken. She had seen him talking to the man next to him before he'd upped his bid once more, and she wondered what that had been all about, though asking him about it wasn't going to make it to her top ten list of things she was curious about during negotiations. There was an entire list of other details burning in her mind that she wanted to clarify.

In the basement dungeon, Mistress Vivienne directed each person who had been auctioned off to one of the tables that were lined up along both sides of the large room.

Following the Mistress's hand gesture, Tamara walked over to the second last table on the left, greeting Master Benjamin, who was already waiting there. As the partner of the club owner, Master Benjamin was a well-known figure in the club, and Tamara liked him immensely.

Rising to greet her, he smiled down at her. "Thank you for being a part of the auction, Tamara. You brought in quite the donation." His wide smile made her blush, an annoying quality of her pale complexion.

Feeling slightly shy all of a sudden, she looked down. "Thank you."

"Did Mistress Vivienne already inform you what is going to happen now?"

She nodded. "We are to have our negotiation here, under supervision, to make sure that everything is properly agreed upon in advance of the time that Master Ken won."

Master Benjamin nodded. "That's right. That's what I'm here for. Each table has a dungeon monitor or senior club member to oversee the negotiations. While we trust all of our members, we believe that because we had a crucial part in bringing all these play partners together, we also want to ensure that everyone is getting the best out of this little Christmas celebration."

He pointed at a chair. "Why don't you take a seat? Master Ken should be down here momentarily."

True to Master Benjamin's words, a second wave of people descended into the dungeon. From her seat, she had a fairly good view of the staircase, so she took the opportunity to observe the dominants now filing into the transformed dungeon. Each person looked around the room, searching for whomever they had purchased during the auction. Then they strode in that direction with the confident body language all dominants seemed to have in common.

It was exciting in the same way it was thrilling to watch nature documentaries about predators stalking their prey. Except this was way sexier.

It didn't take long for Master Ken to appear, and her eyes fixed on him, watching his elegant stride as he directed his steps towards the back of the room, following Mistress Vivienne's directions.

He was handsome in a hard-edged kind of way. Lean and tall, his face showed the straight lines of his cheeks and jaw bones. He'd trimmed his dark hair shorter on the sides and slightly longer on top, styled in a way that suggested he cared about his outer appearance. Not that she figured him to be self-absorbed. She might never have spoken to the man, but she'd heard other submissives describe him as a generous dom, which translated to him giving out orgasms as skilled as the best of them.

That had potential, Tamara thought, and immediately heat crept into her cheeks. Her light complexion really was both a blessing and a curse.

Of course, there was a chance he might care more about his image as a good lover than about the women he was with, but Tamara figured she might as well reserve judgement until she actually met the guy.

Looking around the room as he walked, his eyes met hers and a quick smirk of his lips showed he'd found what he was after.

Her.

As he moved in her direction, Tamara noticed he wasn't alone. The man he had spoken with during the auction walked beside him, a smile playing around his lips.

She looked over to Master Benjamin, but he, too, was watching the two men approach with interest. An uneasy feeling came over her. Somehow, she had the eerie sense that she was missing a crucial piece of information. Something that might bite her in the ass.

Perhaps literally.

When the two men arrived at the table, they both looked at her. Master Ken's smile was that of a man pleased with what he saw, and the intensity of his gaze made her bare toes curl under the table. The man with him had a wide, easy-going smile, though it was still appreciative.

Before she could get up or say anything, Master Ken turned to Master Benjamin.

"Could we have a word?"

Master Benjamin didn't raise an eyebrow, stepping towards the center of the room with the two men. They had a brief conversation, though as much as she tried, Tamara couldn't hear a thing that was being discussed. The only thing that became clear was that she was definitely in for something more than a straightforward limits discussion with Master Ken.

She needed to ask the other submissives who this Master was. Since Andrew worked weekends, they always went to the club on Wednesdays, meaning she rarely met the weekend crowd. But maybe she had heard his name before?

Unfortunately, everyone else in the room was busy with their own negotiations and her phone was in a locker upstairs.

When the three of them returned, Tamara focused on Master Benjamin, expecting him to fill her in on what was going on. Instead, Master Ken spoke. "It is nice to meet you, Tamara. I have seen you in the club and I am delighted that we'll have this opportunity to scene together."

Another unexpected moment of shyness came over her, which was rather strange given the fact she'd just allowed herself to be auctioned off in a kink club. Normally she considered herself comfortable meeting new people, an essential trait in her job, but the way Master Ken looked at her made her feel self-aware somehow.

He wasn't just looking; he was sizing her up. Almost as if he were analyzing her body language and replies more than any other dominant ever had. And dominants tended to be more attentive already.

"It's nice to meet you, too." She couldn't look away from him, drawn in by his focus on her.

His answering smile was gentle, a contrast to his otherwise intense demeanor and sharp features.

"I'm Mater Johnathan," the other man said, finally drawing Tamara's attention away from Master Ken. He was still smiling widely, his eyes sparkling with mischief. "And I am very pleased to meet you, too, Tamara."

Tamara shook his outstretched hand, still sitting awkwardly while the three men towered over her.

Master Johnathan kept her hand in his for a moment, his grip on her gentle but firm. He might look easy-going, but Tamara sensed he was as dominant as Master Ken. Unlike Master Ken, Master Johnathan had blond hair that hung down to just above his shoulders. He also had a bit more than a five o'clock shadow instead of Master Ken's clean-shaven face. But despite the differences, the two looked similar in a way. Maybe because of their facial features that made their cheekbones stand out.

When Master Johnathan released her hand, she tried to get up, feeling uncomfortable and oddly rude to be sitting when everyone else was standing, but Master Benjamin waved his hand, indicating she should stay in place. What was she to do after that but keep her butt in her chair?

She watched as Master Benjamin walked to one of the scene areas and pulled an extra chair over for Master Johnathan, who responded with a grin and a nod.

All three Masters sat down, and Master Benjamin pushed a paper over to Master Ken and Master Johnathan. "I'll need you both to fill one of these out, please. You can get a second copy in the office before you leave."

When the two Masters looked down to read the document, Tamar turned expectantly to Master Benjamin, who smiled at her. "It appears that not one Master, but two have won your auction lot. Masters Ken and Johnathan have combined their bid to win time with you."

Her eyes flicked over to the two men, neither one of whom was looking at the document. Instead, both of them were looking at her.

"Oh?" was all she could get out.

Master Benjamin chuckled. "Indeed. There was no rule against this, so it was completely legitimate. However, it means we'll have to make sure that during the negotiation, we figure out the details of this arrangement."

Ken

"We get you for three days." Master Ken looked over the papers. "It looks like you have no dates marked off as unavailable over the holidays."

Tamara nodded. "That's right. I'm off work and I have no plans over the holidays, so I'm free whenever you would like to see me."

She watched as Master Ken looked over at Johnathan. "Got any plans, cuz? Other than the Christmas dinner?"

That explained why the two looked so similar. Cousins. Why hadn't she heard about Master Ken having a cousin in the club? This was like opening an exam and realizing you had read the wrong chapters of the textbook. Completely unprepared.

Master Johnathan shook his head. "Nope, I'm free anytime. Got some vacation days saved up, too. Your call."

Master Ken nodded. "Then why don't we do the 24th, 25th, and 26th? I wasn't planning on going anywhere on those days, so we might as well make them ours."

Tamara couldn't quite hide her surprise. Most people didn't want to do anything other than be with family on those days. Then again, she supposed the cousins were planning to be together, unless this was some sort of timeshare arrangement.

Damn, she needed to figure out what they were planning.

Was this going to be a threesome? She hadn't considered that when signing up, but the thought sent a thrill down her belly, right to the place where her legs met. She couldn't deny that the thought of those two Masters working together, dominating her, made her brain come up with all sorts of naughty fantasies. In her official club limits list, she had marked threesomes as a point of interest, but she had definitely gotten more than she bargained for in this auction.

Master Benjamin looked over at her. "Those days work for you?"

She nodded. "Yes, sir."

Santa help her. It looked like she was actually getting laid for Christmas.

Master Benjamin made some notes on his paper before looking up again. "Now the question is where and how you want to arrange those three days."

This time, Tamara spoke up first. "I'm free to come to the club on short notice if you want to take my phone number and text me whenever you want me to show up here. I can be at the club within 45 minutes." She smiled, this part she'd come prepared for and it was a forthcoming arrangement.

Unfortunately, she didn't get the expected reaction. Master Ken scowled, while Master Johnathan just looked over at his cousin, grinning, as if he hadn't been this amused in weeks. "Dude, you're making our little subbie nervous."

"Well, we're hardly going to stay three days at the club. As comfortable as I've heard those spanking benches are, I have a feeling that we'll need breaks in between."

While Tamara tried to figure out what Master Ken meant by that, her earlier nerves began resurfacing, and Master Johnathan, watching her now, laughed. Actually laughed out loud, causing the people at the next table to look at them.

"Sorry, my bad," he told them, before leaning back in his chair, still smiling. "Maybe Jessica is going to lend us the harem room."

Unlike Tamara, Master Ken seemed to follow the suggestion with no trouble, and he looked almost contemplative at her. It took about four seconds for the light bulb to turn on and a squeak to escape her lips.

"I thought that throughout the three days you can, you know, message me whenever you want to do a scene. Not that we'd be together for seventy-two hours in a row." Did everyone think that's what she'd offered during the auction? The thought alone was making her body ache. Except she could also feel a strange tingle inside of her.

She wasn't a masochist. Surely the thought of three full days of going at it wasn't making her horny?

All three dominance looked at her, then Master Benjamin laughed.

Oh god, was that why Master Ken and Master Johnathan had combined their bid? So they could take turns with her and rest in between?

"Tamara, you offered three days when you signed up for the auction. I'm pretty sure that Masters Ken and Johnathan want to make those three days count. Is that going to be a problem?" While his voice was gentle and his question sounded reasonable, Master Benjamin couldn't quite hide his amusement.

Heat rose to her cheeks, and she shook her head quickly. She had offered three days, and as appalling as that seemed right now, she wasn't going to back out and risk losing the huge donation that her auction slot had brought in for the women's shelter. "No, no, it's not going to be a problem. I mean, I'm obviously available for whatever you want. It's what I put up for the auction. It's just... I guess I just hadn't expected to stay at the club for three days, but I'll do it, of course." She was rambling, and now all three of them were grinning at her, even Master Ken.

Master Ken looked at Master Benjamin. "There's no rule that we have to stick to the club, is there?"

Master Benjamin shook his head. "No, it's up to the participants and their comfort level. You can arrange for whatever you want to do. It's your scenes, or, in this case, days." He said the last part with a wink at Tamara, making her face burn even hotter. "Of course, all participants need to be okay with whatever arrangement you come up with, and I am here to ensure that's the case."

Feeling his eyes on her, Tamara looked at Master Ken and met his intense stare. It felt like she was about to take some sort of test.

"I would like for you to stay the three days in my home. Provided that you're comfortable with that idea. You're welcome to come to the house before with someone else to look around and you're more than welcome to vet me further, before you make your decision. We can also arrange for someone else in the club to phone in regularly to make sure that you're feeling safe and taken care of."

Her head spun slightly at the idea. She could stay at Master Ken's house for three days. Over Christmas. She would not be alone at Christmas at all. The idea was nice, if a bit scary.

She looked over at Master Johnathan. "Will you be staying there, too?"

Johnathan nodded. "There's two guest rooms. I might as well. Seems like it's the most convenient place to go. Certainly wouldn't work out in my apartment."

Master Ken scoffed. "You've really got to get yourself a bigger place."

For a second Tamara wondered what Master Ken would say about her little sardine can of an apartment, but then her brain focused back on the decision at hand.

Master Benjamin wouldn't allow this if he didn't consider both Masters to be trustworthy people. Plus, a ton of club members had seen Master Ken win her at the auction, providing another thin layer of protection. "I think I'll be okay with going to your place. I'd like to do some vetting and know the address in advance though, please. I know Jessica vetted you already, but it would ease my mind to get some references before I commit. I would also appreciate the safety calls. I'm sure my friend Casey and her husband, Master Andrew, will be happy to do it."

Benjamin smiled, making more notes on his sheet of paper. "Perfect. I will make sure that I'll check in with them, and, just to be extra safe, I'll also take over a couple of the check-in calls myself. We'll set up a schedule for those."

Tamara nodded her agreement. That would be more than enough to make her feel safe. In all reality, it was probably more than what was truly needed, but she also wasn't stupid. If someone offered her a thick safety net, she was going to take it.

"Now, let's chat scene limits," Master Benjamin suggested, and Master Johnathan leaned forward, looking like he was a kid about to decide on the Christmas candy he wanted to try out first.

"I believe we should discuss what Tamara feels comfortable with when it comes to being with two doms at the same time." Master Ken's reasonable tone was almost drowned out by the sound of her heart beating loudly in her chest.

This was actually happening. The thought made a nervous laugh bubble out. Maybe she needed to add some anal plugs to her advents calendar to get ready.

Chapter Four

December 23rd

Ken

As was the case each year, more than his normal load of patient appointments had piled up as it neared Christmas. While people liked to refer to this time of year as magical, it was, in all reality, filled with a never ending amount of familial trauma. Yet another reason to dislike this season.

Sitting in his home office to finish saving his reflections on an unscheduled phone call with a patient, Ken stared out the window. No car was coming down the street yet. For the best. He needed a few minutes to step back from his work.

That call had hit a bit too close to home. A grieving thirty-year-old preparing to celebrate her first Christmas without her mother, who had passed away in the summer. He felt for her, which was why he'd accepted the call outside his usual hours. Not that she'd realized the odd hour in her state of mind.

Why did people have to place so much stock on this holiday? Religion certainly didn't account for the consumerist extravagance associated with it.

He wasn't obtuse enough to miss that he had his own problems to sort through, and his quarterly sessions with his own therapist certainly helped him be more cognizant of that, but if his dislike for one holiday in a calendar year was the worst of his hang-ups, Ken figured he was doing pretty damn well.

And this year he'd taken steps to cheer himself up.

Again, he looked out his window and finally he spotted a car pull into his driveway.

His contentment with the decision to move past his yearly dark patch with the help of a certain Club B submissive was disrupted when Tamara got out of her car.

It had been three weeks since their auction arrangements and he hadn't been able to go to Club B since, filling his Saturdays and evenings with sessions for patients who needed him. If he had seen her since then, maybe he would have been able to tell her she should not bring any Christmas decorations to his home.

The thought was so ridiculous it hadn't even occurred to him. Who brought decorations to someone else's house?

Tamara looked up at him, her eyes wide with excitement. They matched the color of the damned tree.

What had she been thinking? Then again, it wasn't exactly normal to spend your holidays at the house of an almost stranger. With all his usual foresight, his preoccupation with work had meant he hadn't been as prepared for Tamara's arrival as he would have liked to be.

And now she was walking to his door with a freaking miniature Christmas tree, including a plastic ornament of an elf.

Sighing, he opened the door. "Tamara, hello."

Tamara's smile was genuine, and he felt almost guilty at his irritation with her. "Hey."

"Let me help you with your bag."

She put the Christmas tree down and let the bag slide down her shoulder, handing it over to him. It was a duffel bag stuffed to its capacity; the seams stretching around the zipper.

Noticing the way he looked at her luggage, she chuckled. "I wasn't sure what the next three days would entail, so I packed some of my club clothes, normal stuff, and, of course, a Christmas sweater." She grinned up at him, and he tried to control his scowl, though from her confused look he figured he hadn't been very successful.

Hopefully, she didn't expect this to be some sort of kinky holiday celebration. What he needed was to get away from everything and allow himself to have a good time.

"Well, let me show you to your room so you can unpack." He turned and held the door open for her. She gave him another smile, though this one seemed a bit more hesitant than the last. He really needed to get his act together before he scared the poor subbie off.

Trying to ignore the Christmas tree she had picked up again, he led her through the hallway and up the stairs that led to the second floor. Turning right, he opened the last door on the left. Before walking through, he nodded at the door opposite. "That is the bathroom. Unfortunately, it's not connected to your room, but it will be yours alone to use during the next three days, so you can spread out your things as much as you want."

This seemed to amuse her, her eyes twinkling, though she only nodded, following him into the bigger of his two guest rooms. His housekeeper had been in yesterday and set up the room and bathroom for a visitor, though it was apparent from the stuffed animals and board games on one dresser that his nieces were the ones who usually stayed in the room.

Technically, Mellie and Cora were his second cousins, not his nieces, but as he'd grown up alongside Johnathan and his sister Felicia, he viewed Felicia's daughters as his nieces and they called him uncle Ken.

"The room is great, thank you," Tamara said, drawing his attention back to her. She was still holding the damn tree and looked uncertain, despite her polite words.

Get your shit together, Ken.

"You can put your tree over there," he offered, pointing at a low side table standing in a corner of the room next to an armchair. If she kept it there, at least it would be out of sight and he could move on with the next three days without constantly having to fight his own grouchiness.

"That's perfect," Tamara exclaimed, looking more comfortable as she walked over and carefully placed the tree there. He figured a plastic tree hardly warranted being treated so carefully, but once again, he chose not to comment. Instead, he watched as Tamara took a step back, admiring the thing. "It looks great next to the red chair, don't you think?"

He gave what he hoped to be an affirmative sounding grunt.

"Why don't I give you a few minutes to unpack and settle in? I'll cook some dinner and you can come down whenever you're ready."

Tamara turned around. "Thank you. I'll do that."

Downstairs, he started chopping up vegetables for the stew. He'd been looking forward to the next three days ever since winning the auction, and found the prospect of co-topping with Johnathan only heightened his anticipation. They'd only done it twice before, and the experience had been great. Unfortunately, their schedules meant they often attended the club on different days, Johnathan on the weekends when the large crowd meant he could mingle and be social, while Ken went on Wednesdays when a smaller crowd and more intense scenes meant he could enjoy the club without the pressure of constant small talk.

Once his cousin Felicia had told him it was a miracle that a man as introverted and terse as him had become a psychologist, but his aunt had walked over saying that his choice of work hadn't surprised her for a second, since none of Ken's patients would ever doubt Ken's sincerity when he spoke with them. He had a seriousness and gravity to him that resonated with people. His aunt's words always pulled him through when he worked with particularly challenging patients.

By the time the stew was simmering, he heard Tamara walk down the stairs. He looked up with anticipation.

After some consideration, instead of having her arrive the morning of Christmas Eve, he'd invited her to arrive on the evening of the 23rd so they could ease into their time together. They had informed Benjamin, who'd arranged the safety calls and paperwork. He had the next three days to fully enjoy the little subbie, until she would leave on the 26th in the evening, leaving Johnathan free to attend their grandmother's Christmas dinner.

It was time to get into the spirit of things.

At least that's how he felt until Tamara walked into the kitchen wearing a damn Rudolph the reindeer sweater.

How the hell was his dick going to work when confronted with that?

Tamara

Things were not starting off the way she'd expected. Somehow, when she'd imagined arriving at Ken's place, she'd pictured herself walking in, met by desire-ridden Masters Ken and Johnathan, who'd quickly strip her of her clothes, ignoring her belongings and ravishing her right there in the hallway.

She had to admit that while being shown to her guest room and being given some time to settle in was kind, she couldn't help feeling disappointed. Especially since Master Ken seemed to be in a less than enthusiastic mood.

Not that he was rude or anything, just not as excited as she was.

Trying to ignore his scowl, she stepped further into the kitchen. "It smells great in here."

He finally blinked and swiveled his head to look toward the stove. "Thank you. I'm making a vegetable stew. I hope that suits you?"

If it hadn't been to her liking, it would have been a bit too late now, anyway, but luckily a stew sounded perfect. Maybe it would warm Master Ken up to her a bit more, so she smiled and nodded. "Yes, that sounds great. Will we be eating alone?" She'd expected Master Johnathan to be here already.

"Johnathan gets off work late, but he should be here soon and join us for dinner."

"What does he do?" she asked, happy for the opportunity to find out a bit more about the men whom she'd spend the holidays with.

"Why don't I get us some drinks and we'll sit down in the living room? Then I'll tell you," Master Ken asked, and she readily agreed.

With a glass of red wine in hand, Tamara followed Ken into the living room and looked around, finding the room completely bare of any Christmas decorations. "You haven't put your decorations up yet?" she asked, surprised. "Are you working long hours, too?"

Master Ken's eyebrows drew together as if her question bothered him. Today, he didn't match the image she'd built of him after their encounter at the auction at all. Nor did he match the descriptions of the submissives she'd spoken to while vetting him. They'd described him as caring, intelligent, and utterly skilled as a dom. Instead, he seemed closed off to her.

Was he always this moody? That would make the next three days a lot less fun than what she'd hoped.

At least Master Johnathan seemed to be a pleasant, easy-going person, so she had that to look forward to.

Finally, he answered, as if he'd had to contemplate his words. "I don't decorate for Christmas. I don't really enjoy the holiday."

He was an actual Grinch.

Tamara could feel her excitement about her time in his house fade further with each minute she spent here. She'd hoped to have a holiday she could enjoy with others, not being alone for once. Instead, it looked like Master Ken would do his damnedest to prevent any Christmas spirit from entering his house. Only an internal reminder about the women's shelter that would benefit from her sacrifice made her nod and sit down without sharing her thoughts out loud.

She might be sad about his lack of a Christmas spirit, but she could still have a good time. Master Ken had an amazing reputation as a dom, so they could have a different kind of fun. And with Master Johnathan there, she was sure they could still turn these three days into a success.

She took a sip of the delicious wine and met Master Ken's eyes. "So, you were going to tell me what you and Johnathan do for a living."

His small smile drew her eyes to his full lips. "I'm a psychologist, primarily working with people who are working through grief and long-term traumas."

He leaned back, leaning one very well-defined arm over the back of the two-seater. Whatever he was lacking in holiday joy, he was making up for in being hot as hell. And, obviously, brains.

She leaned forward. The evening might not have started off as she'd hoped, but the others must have been right. The dom across from her must be smart and caring if he'd ended up a psychologist. Time to find out what he'd come up with for their time together.

Chapter Five

December 23rd

Johnathan

Johnathan let himself into his cousin's house and followed the sound of voices into the living room. Ken and Tamara were sitting and talking, though it was apparent that the mood was not the one he'd expected. Given his cousin's determination to win time with Tamara, he'd half expected them already going at it.

Not that Ken didn't have the self-control of a saint, but that wouldn't have stopped him from welcoming his house guest in a much more intense way on any other day. Or at least, that was what Johnathan had thought he was going to walk in on.

Instead, the two seemed to have a pleasant, if somewhat formal, conversation going on. Not the most exciting start to their time together.

"Hello you two," he greeted, stepping into the room.

The way Tamara's eyes brightened when she saw him made another red flag pop into his head. She didn't look like a woman having the best of times. On the other hand, the appreciative way her eyes roamed over his body told him this wasn't a lost cause just yet.

"Hey, Johnathan," Ken greeted him. "Dinner will be ready in five minutes. I imagine you're starving?"

Johnathan laughed. "Always. I'll just drop my bag upstairs."

"You've got Cora's room," Ken called after him, making Johnathan grin. His nieces loved their sleepovers at Ken's place and they had insisted that the guest rooms were not, in fact, guest rooms, but rather Mellie's and Cora's very own personal bedrooms away from home.

Heading to the smaller of the two bedrooms, Johnathan dropped his bag and turned to head back down. Looked like it was best not to leave those two to their own devices for much longer, and luckily he had showered at work, so he didn't need to worry about smelling like a wet dog. Training military dogs was the best job he could have ever hoped for, but it came with the side effect that on most days he needed to take more showers than the average person.

He found the others in the kitchen. Tamara was setting the table, while Ken stirred a stew. It was an oddly homey scene, and the calm of it felt surprisingly pleasant. Definitely a step up from going home to his crummy apartment.

"I'm starving," he announced.

"That's good, because it looks like Ken has cooked enough for an entire army."

Johnathan chuckled. It looked like Tamara hadn't lost her good humor despite the strange stiffness from the earlier conversation he'd walked in on. Still, he raised an eyebrow at his cousin, who understood immediately.

"I told Tamara to skip titles until after dinner. Then we can reassess what we want to do with the evening."

The way Ken's eyes moved over Tamara showed his cousin was hungry for more than stew. Good. Looked like with a nudge in the right direction, this evening had the potential to turn into the night he'd been looking forward to.

"Fair enough." He walked over to the fridge and pulled out the butter. "You have rolls?"

Ken grinned. "In the oven."

Tamara looked between them. "Am I missing something?"

Johnathan chuckled. "Nan, our grandmother, insists that a dinner isn't a complete meal without rolls. Really, any meal requires a certain amount of carbs, ideally coming from bread, in her opinion."

Tamara smiled. "Sounds like a sensible woman."

"Most of the time," Ken said as he served the stew.

Johnathan sat to Tamara's left, while Ken took the chair to her right. They left the chair across from her empty, and Johnathan enjoyed watching the little subbie as she took in how they had boxed her in. She reacted nicely to such a subtle maneuver, which was promising. There was nothing more fun than subtle foreplay. Well, except the actual play, of course.

Ken raised his wine glass. "Enjoy."

As Tamara raised her first spoonful to her mouth, Johnathan allowed himself a moment to admire her lips. Unlike the rest of her, her mouth was anything but innocent looking. With her blond waves and porcelain skin, she had pulled off the angel dress easily, but instead of the pale pink lipstick she'd worn the day of the auction, her natural lips were a beautiful red.

"What made you sign up for the auction?" he asked. "Other than the obvious charity aspect."

Tamara laughed. "Isn't that enough motivation?"

It might have been a reprimand, had there not been a twinkle in her eyes.

"Sure, but I figure you were hoping to get more out of it. That's certainly true for me. What about you, cuz?"

Ken grinned. "Yup, definitely in it for more than the donation. I could have donated directly otherwise. This is bound to be more fun!'"

The way Tamara's cheeks colored was beautiful and her chuckle was equally attractive. "Fair enough, you got me. I'm a naughty kinkster who doesn't have a ton of spare change to just donate, and this way I got the best of both worlds. I got to help do some good and I'm getting a fun Christmas treat for myself all in one."

"So we're your Christmas treats, are we?" Johnathan teased.

None of them were eating anymore, and the sexual tension in the room grew with each passing moment. Stew just didn't have a chance to win out over that.

Instead of answering, Tamara nodded, smiling shyly. Her Christmas treats indeed.

"Why don't we move to the living room, then?" Kens suggested, his voice having grown rough, making Johnathan grin. Yeah, his cuz was on the same page as he was.

"Yes, sir," Tamara agreed, falling seamlessly into the right headspace for a scene.

Tamara

Tamara wanted to sigh in relief. Ever since Master Johnathan had arrived, the mood had lightened. Even Master Ken now seemed to be a lot more interested in doing the things she was here for. After all, he'd been the one to suggest abandoning their food to move into the living room.

Finally.

Her body tingled with excitement. She had never been with two men, not to speak of two Masters. Being nervous didn't even begin to describe her state of mind right now, and yet she was glad they were getting started.

Maybe she should feel ashamed of how much she wanted to get kinky, but the anticipation was killing her. After they got started, she would surely be able to relax more.

"If Tamara thinks we're her treat, why don't we start with a little get to know each other exercise? She might as well get a taste for what she's about to get for the next three days." Master Ken's gaze on her was smoldering as he made his suggestion. Something had changed, and she wasn't about to complain.

Master Johnathan's nod was accompanied by a chuckle. "Lets."

The two men moved to the leather couch, opening their buttons and zippers before sitting down. While they were both wearing jeans, Master Ken's were black whereas Master Johnathan's were a faded blue that looked almost white in areas. Light and dark, like their moods and hair. And yet, Tamara couldn't say she was more drawn to one over the other. Not when they were both staring at her with desire in their eyes.

Her start with Master Ken had been a bit rocky today, but he was everything she'd ever craved in a Master. He had that intensity about him that gave her goosebumps when she pictured him using it to get her to do the things he desired. Master Johnathan, on the other hand, was easy to be with. He made her feel at ease and more willing to try something new.

Like giving blow jobs to two men at the same time.

She stared at the two men for a second, realizing that both their cocks had sprung loose from their pants, standing at attention for her. Ready to be tasted.

Her own personal Christmas treat. She wanted to giggle, but that didn't seem advisable while staring at the pride and joy of two well-established BDSM Masters.

"Why don't you get started with Ken," Master Johnathan suggested. His voice was gentle, but laced with amusement. "And if you don't mind, you can use your hand on me, so I don't feel left out." It wasn't so much a suggestion as an order, and her body responded with needs of its own. That would have to wait.

Prompted by Master Johnathan's words, Tamara looked up at Master Ken, whose lazy smile told her he was waiting to see what she was going to do. With him, it felt almost like a challenge. Remembering that it had been him who had been bidding on time with her first, she smiled and leaned forward.

She pressed her lips against the tip of his cock, wanting to start gently, but as she touched him, his dick twitched, escaping her lips. Furrowing her brows, she leaned in even closer, until the top of her head touched Master Ken's belly, and captured his dick in her mouth, sucking him in.

His moan was a reward for her determination and she moved her lips up and down his shaft, tasting him for the first time. His smell was woodsy and the salty taste of him reminded her of her favorite salted caramel candies.

As far as Christmas treats went, Master Ken was perfect.

As she found a slow rhythm, easing into the blow job, her right hand searched out Master Johnathan. As she closed her hand around his shaft, she could feel the heat emanating from him. His cock was veinier than his cousin's, and she could feel the pulsing of his desire against her palm.

It was intoxicating

She began moving her hand, quickly realizing that the easiest way to do this was to move her hand in the opposite direction to her mouth. Each time she let her lips slide down Master Ken's dick, taking him as deep as her position allowed, she moved her hand up Master Johnathan's cock, swirling her thumb over the tip.

With her rhythm established, she moved back a bit, allowing her to look up at Master Ken, who was smiling down at her. It was a genuinely pleased smile this time, and a knot of worry that had remained after his terse welcome loosened.

Her tongue traced against his shaft now, as the tip of his cock hit a different spot at the back of her throat. It wasn't exactly comfortable, but the way Master Ken's eyes hooded each time his tip touched against her made her want to do it more. She would show him how good these next three days could be.

This was her celebration, and giving these two Masters pleasure would be her special gift back to them.

Ken

Sitting on his couch, receiving oral from the cute sub, was pretty high on his list of things he could get used to. She was generous, taking him deep and showing her pleasure with little moans and the slight deepening of the color in her cheeks.

She was damned good, too.

As her lips slid up and down his cock, he finally felt himself relax. It had been a rough few weeks, but this was exactly what he'd wanted for the next few days. That, and spoiling a sweet little subbie a little. Anything to embrace the positive things in life.

Johnathan's leg touched against his own, which may have been strange under different circumstances, but it was not only hard to care about any weirdness when you were getting fucking good oral, but it also reminded him of the possibilities for the next few days.

They had topped together in the club a few times, and it had been good. Great, actually. But there was one thing they hadn't yet done together, and Tamara hadn't made it off limits during their pre-scene discussion. Her pretty ass was on the table, and that meant he and Johnathan could have a lot of fun they hadn't enjoyed together before.

All his thoughts scattered when Tamara's teeth gently scraped against the top side of his dick. His eyes sprung open, and he looked at her, meeting her sparkling eyes. The way the corners of her eyes crinkled told him she'd very much done it on purpose, probably to ensure his attention was fully on her.

Little minx.

Looked like he had to remind her who was in charge of things.

Chapter Six

December 23rd

Ken

"No teeth. And I want you to suck now," Ken ordered, watching as Tamara's pupils dilated with his order.

Yeah, she wanted his attention on her. Wanted his control.

She got to work with enthusiasm, hollowing her cheeks as she sucked him off.

Enforcing their dynamic, he placed his hand on the back of her head, guiding her movements. The feeling of her warmth around his cock combined with the gentle tugging of her lips made his balls draw up. He had a decent control over himself and could have drawn this out, but Tamara had more work to do today, so he leaned back and said, "faster."

She did as she was told, and he could feel his release building.

Without having to direct her, she used her tongue to tease the tip of his cock each time she pulled back, before taking him deep again. Then she pursed her lips tighter and took him even deeper. It was everything he needed.

"Swallow it," he ordered, and hot semen shot up his shaft and into her mouth.

Tamara swallowed and gently licked the tip of his cock to clean him off. It was such a sweet gesture that he leaned forward and gave her a kiss on the lips. "You did good. I hope you liked your treat."

Tamara nodded, looking up at him through her tinted lashes.

He hadn't been wrong to follow Andrew's advice and make use of the opportunity the auction presented. His instincts about Tamara being a generous and sweet submissive were proving to be correct.

"Good, because there is more waiting for you," he said, nodding over to Johnathan, who'd been waiting patiently.

"Yes, sir," Tamara said, her voice husky.

Looked like she was getting off on doing this.

Perhaps he could help that along a bit more. After all, she'd done a fine job of pleasing him. It would be a shame if he didn't get to have a taste.

As Tamara scooted over to Johnathan's lap, still on her knees, Ken rose.

At Johnathan's questioning look, Ken nodded down at the little subbie and Johnathan gave him a crooked smile, nodding his understanding.

As he stepped behind her and moved the living room table out of the way, Tamara turned around, watching him with wide eyes.

"Tamara."

Johnathan's command forced her attention back to him.

Ken grinned to himself. This was even more fun than he'd remembered. With Tamara's lips now firmly closed around Johnathan's cock, she had no way of watching what he was doing, and wasn't that a nice way of being able to surprise a good little girl?

He went down on the ground, taking hold of Tamara's legs, and gently moved them apart. He could see that Johnathan had placed his hand on Tamara's head, ensuring she stayed busy with her task.

When he had her in the position he wanted, he took a pillow from the adjacent armchair and put it on the floor before lying down on his back, his head now between Tamara's legs.

Time to have a little treat of his own.

As his tongue slid over her, her whimper was like kindling to a fire. Pushing in deeper, he tasted her, allowing himself to enjoy the tangy flavor.

He could feel her rhythmic movements as she worked over his cousin, and he matched her pace, swirling his tongue around her clit in gentle strokes that had her press herself against him.

Damn, he loved the way she didn't hold back, showing him what she liked. Too many submissives were worried that showing a dom what they enjoyed meant they were taking control away from him, when, to him, this was the sweetest way for a sub to compliment him. And he had no intention of giving up his control, so that shouldn't be a concern of hers, anyway.

Instead, he pushed his tongue into her, holding on to her legs to direct her movements, getting her to ride his face. It took her a moment to let go of thinking she needed to hold herself up and match his movements. Finally, her leg muscles went limp, allowing him to move her up and down.

Luckily, his work frustrations meant he'd been spending a decent amount of time in the gym, working through his emotions before he was ready to head home in the evenings. The built up strength now worked in his favor as he supported Tamara's weight, allowing her to focus on Johnathan while he worked to get her closer to her own release.

Changing his tactic, he placed his lips around her clit, sucking. Long, long, short. And again. Then he swirled around her sensitive nub, finding her leaning into him each time he pressed down over the top.

That was her sweet spot, apparently. He could work with that.

Repeating the pattern, he made sure to linger over the top each time a little longer, wiggling his tongue and driving her need up. As her moaning got louder and she moved her hips to get more friction, he lapped over her before pressing against her nub and gently flicking his tongue against her again and again.

"Focus darling," Johnathan ordered, and Ken could feel Tamara's pussy clenching at the order.

He backed off a bit, moving slower and allowing her to ride his tongue while she increased her own rhythm to please Johnathan.

"Like that," Johnathan said, and Tamara pressed herself against his face, the praise driving her own desire higher.

Well, then.

As Tamara worked her magic, his cousin's breathing grew more labored, and it didn't take long before he ordered Tamara to swallow.

As her movements slowed, Ken picked up his own, focusing all his attentions on the most sensitive of spots he'd discovered. Her moans were needy and demanding, the sound the perfect soundtrack for his treat.

Tamara's weight moved off of him then. Apparently Johnathan had taken over holding her, probably pulling her upper body into his lap to give her support. It meant Ken's hands were now free, and he entered her with two fingers, twisting to feel for the telltale bumpy patch in her smooth depth.

She was swollen, which helped him find the raised area quickly. Massaging her in gentle circles, he matched the movement of his tongue to that of his fingers and could feel her pussy clench around him as she flew higher towards her release.

With one last flick of his tongue, her control shattered and her pussy constricted against him in waves, trying to wring as much pleasure as she could get out of him.

She deserved it.

This was about to be a few delightful days for them.

Johnathan

With Tamara upstairs taking a shower, Johnathan followed Ken into the kitchen to clean up the remnants of their dinner. They might have to offer the little subbie something later to make sure she didn't go hungry after they'd cut dinner short, but Johnathan couldn't bring himself to feel anything but content with the way the evening had worked out so far.

"What do you think?" he asked Ken while he collected plates and brought them to the dishwasher.

"I like her," Ken said. "She's a sweet one, the way she submits."

Johnathan had to agree. It was obvious Tamara reveled in following orders and trying to please them. And she gave amazing head, despite the added challenge of being distracted by his cousin's efforts to drive her crazy.

"Are you going to tell me what made you want to bid on her in the first place?"

Ken smiled. "I was wondering when you'd get around to asking me that."

Sometimes having a psychologist in the family meant being subjected to their behavioral analysis, but that had never bothered him.

"So?" he prompted, ignoring Ken's comment completely.

"I've seen her scene at the club and she's obviously beautiful," Ken said. "But she's also kind of elusive. I've never seen her hang around and mingle much, so I didn't get a chance to make her a scene offer."

Not surprising. While his cousin couldn't be described as shy by any means, he also didn't enjoy excessive socializing, which could impede his options of casually approaching new play partners. Johnathan put the last glass in the dishwasher and looked at Ken. "That can hardly be the only reason you went to that auction, though."

He let that sentence hang in the air. If Ken wanted to play with someone, he would find a way to approach them one way or another, even if it wasn't convenient. Plus, they both knew that it wasn't like Ken to show up anywhere that was Christmas themed. Talk about a psychologist with his own hang-ups.

Ken's smile was self-deprecating. "Probably not. Could be I overheard her best friend and Andrew chatting about her. I got intrigued."

WRAPPED UP IN LOVE

Now they were getting somewhere. "What did you overhear?"

"That she seems to not only match my kinks, but that we may have similar long-term interests."

Some of the elation the blow job had given him evaporated. "Please tell me this isn't some sort of test whether she's girlfriend material? That's messed up."

"I didn't say that," Ken said, though he put little fervor into his words.

Johnathan shook his head. "You can't be serious."

"Relax. We'll just enjoy the next few days and see what happens. It's not like I'm planning on getting married this year." Ken grinned, but Johnathan sensed there was more to Ken's words than his cousin was actually saying. Every year around Christmas, he started acting out of character, and no one in the family blamed him for it, but this was definitely new.

They finished cleaning up and moved back to the living room, when Tamara came down the stairs. Her hair was still damp, and she wore pajama bottoms with a silky looking top that almost demanded to be felt.

Moving over to her, Johnathan slid his arm around her. "Why don't we sit down and Ken can get us some drinks?"

Ken laughed. "I guess I am the host. Would you like something alcoholic or a hot chocolate?"

Tamara perked up. "A hot chocolate sounds amazing. Would you like some help?"

Ken shook his head at her. "Why don't you and Johnathan chat? It won't take me long."

Turning to Johnathan, Ken raised an eyebrow. "And for you?"

"Hot chocolate sounds good to me. I might need the extra sugar to keep my energy levels up."

Tamara's slightly flushed cheeks deepened even further. Yes, that extra sugar was definitely a good idea.

Chapter Seven

December 23rd

Tamara

"What would you usually be doing on Christmas?" Master Johnathan asked as they waited for their hot chocolates.

She was feeling relaxed after her orgasm and shower, but the material of her silky chemise was moving over her nipples in a distracting way. Getting off always did that to her boobs, and today she would embrace it. She was feeling good, and that was all that mattered.

It didn't hurt that Master Johnathan was smiling openly. "Honestly? On Christmas Eve, I usually like to go for a long hike and then I start my Christmas movie marathon."

"By yourself?" Master Johnathan asked, not hiding his curiosity.

Tamara laughed. "I do a ton of Christmasy stuff with my friends leading up to the twenty-fifth. You know, Christmas markets, crafts fairs, concerts, and that sort of thing. Christmas itself though everyone is with their families, and since I don't have any siblings that means it's just me, myself, and I. It's okay, though, it's always been that way, so it's really not a big deal to me. I get lots of delicious junk food that I only eat once a year and make a couple of lazy days out of it."

She smiled at Johnathan, not wanting any pity. Maybe it wasn't perfect, but she'd turned a holiday that could have really sucked into something that she embraced whole-heartedly.

"So, are Christmas PJs a thing for you then?" Johnathan asked, his crooked grin on display once more.

She grinned back at him, marveling at how it could be so easy to hang out with someone she'd just met. Yeah, he'd known the perfect way to react to her confession.

"They most definitely are. So are Christmas sweaters."

Johnathan laughed. "It's good they didn't put that on your auction sheet."

She drew her eyebrows together. "Why's that?"

Johnathan's eyes flitted to the kitchen, where Ken had just turned on the microwave. "Let's just say my cousin isn't a huge Christmas person." He delivered his explanation without his previous humor, and somehow his shift in mood made an uneasy feeling sink into her gut.

Letting her eyes travel around the room, bare of decorations, she said, "That much seems obvious." Then, recalling Master Ken's earlier mood, Tamara suddenly had the sinking realization that her worry about having done something wrong had actually been on point. "So he probably didn't appreciate that I brought a Christmas tree, eh?"

Johnathan stared at her for a second, before shaking his head. "Did you seriously? I probably should have warned you."

Feeling heat rise to her cheeks, Tamara nodded. "It's just a small, fake one."

"He's taken his dislike for decorations a bit to the extreme, that's for sure."

Who knew a Christmas tree could ever be something offensive? She guessed she was lucky she hadn't brought along her Candy Cane vibrator. She pulled that one out every year on the twenty-fifth for some fun and giggles. The thing had some intense settings, too.

"When I first got my apartment, I didn't have a ton of money, and it's a pretty small place, so while I would have loved to get a real tree each year, I figured it was more sensible to get a small, fake one that I could re-use and it just kind of grew on me over the years."

The thought of not being able to look at it this year hadn't sat right with her, so she'd brought it along, figuring there would be some corner she could put it in. Somehow, having the tree with her felt like a source of strength. Now, apparently, it had turned into something she'd done that would bother Master Ken.

Well, damn.

Easy for Master Johnathan to laugh. He hadn't gotten grumpy Grinch instead of sexy dom earlier. Though at least Master Ken had gotten over it, eventually.

Apparently noticing her growing discomfort, Johnathan took her hand in his. "Look, don't worry about it. It's the holidays. You should have a Christmas tree if it makes you happy."

At that moment, Master Ken walked in carrying two mugs. His eyes immediately landed on their locked hands, and he smiled. He didn't seem to hold a grudge.

Her mind snapped to the way he'd driven her to orgasm with his tongue alone earlier, and she almost blushed. Yes, no grudges.

After retrieving his own drink from the kitchen, Master Ken took a seat in the remaining armchair, looking at her and Johnathan on the couch. "My apologies for not starting our time together off in the best mood," he acknowledged. "It's been a stressful week at work and I let things pile up, letting it out on you earlier."

Had he overheard them?

Tamara tried to hide her surprise. Dominants were known to aim for open communication, but she hadn't expected Master Ken to be so forthright about his grumpy mood earlier. For a moment she considered apologizing for bringing her tree, but decided against it. She really had done nothing wrong. Instead, she smiled at Master Ken, hoping to show she didn't hold it against him.

"It's all right. You were perfectly polite and I think things turned around." She grinned at the thought of just how well things had turned around.

Master Ken's stern features relaxed slightly as he allowed a small smile to play around his lips. "Indeed."

"So, should we discuss what we want to do tomorrow?" Johnathan asked, making sure they didn't linger on anything too heavy.

While she appreciated how easy it was being around Johnathan, she also felt a little disappointed. If Johnathan hadn't rushed to change the topic, could she have asked Master Ken why he'd been in a bad mood? What had happened at work to make it so stressful? And why did he not like Christmas?

Unlike her, Master Ken seemed happy enough to change the topic, leaning back and stretching his legs out. "Jessica is keeping the Club open until nine thirty tomorrow. It's an early closing time, but we could head in and do a scene there?" The way he caught her eyes in his gaze made her body want to melt into a puddle at his feet.

She was already nodding before she'd given any thought to his words.

Johnathan agreed, too. "Yeah, I could check online if we can reserve one of the theme rooms?"

Ken nodded. "Do it. We can surprise Tamara with which one."

Tamara pushed her lower lip forward. "What if I'd like to know now?"

Ken grinned, though his voice was firm. "Well, that would just be too bad for you, wouldn't it?"

This teasing side of him, mixed with the stern Master beneath it, was better than any aphrodisiac.

"Tamara was saying she enjoys going for hikes on Christmas Eve. I was thinking we should do that."

Something about Master Johnathan's tone told Tamara there was more behind his statement than simply wanting to do something nice for her by doing the thing she'd told him she enjoyed. Given the nature of their arrangement, that feeling probably wasn't far off, especially since it was Master Ken's turn to chuckle. The noise was insanely hot, a rough rumble that seemed to vibrate right through her, and suddenly her earlier orgasm and shower weren't enough to keep the heat of desire from rising in her again.

And then there was the silky chemise still sliding over her nipples like the tease of fabric it was.

Master Johnathan let go of her hand, instead placing it on her thigh. Immediately, Tamara hoped he'd let it travel higher, relieving some of her rousing desire. Unfortunately, he kept it firmly in place.

"You want to take her out into the woods?" Master Ken asked, clearly amused, but also somehow sounding as if he didn't think it was a good idea.

"Not exactly. I was thinking we could go to Felicia's and Garret's place."

Tamara studied Master Ken's face. She would bet her tiny tree that he could keep his expressions neutral in front of submissives if he wanted to hide his thoughts. In his own home, though, he might be more likely to allow his actual reactions to show. In fact, right now, he looked like he was struggling with wanting to reject the idea, but also intrigued by the possibilities Johnathan's suggestion had sparked.

"Who are Felicia and Garret, and what kind of place do they have that we could hike there?" Perhaps they were talking about a farm outside of Toronto? Leaving the city sounded perfect. Since she was reliant on public transportation, she rarely got the chance to leave, unless she carpooled with Casey and Andrew to Club B, which was a forty-five-minute drive outside of the city. Of course, that was always in the late evening, so it had been a while since she'd actually done a day trip.

"Felicia is Johnathan's sister and Garret is her husband," Master Ken answered in a dry voice. "And they have a Christmas-tree farm."

The way he said it told Tamara two things. Master Ken was fond of his female cousin, and he couldn't quite bring himself to dislike the farm, even though it was Christmas related.

Perhaps there was a chance for her tiny tree yet.

Noticing her look, Master Ken raised an eyebrow. "Yes, I'm not a fan of Christmas, but even I have to admit that the Christmas-tree farm is beautiful. It's a suitable spot for what Johnathan has in mind, anyway."

He accompanied the end of his little speech with a look at his cousin. A look that expressed he himself wasn't opposed to whatever Master Johnathan had in mind.

"And what exactly do you have in mind?" She turned to the grinning man next to her.

WRAPPED UP IN LOVE

"I think it'll be more fun if we explain that tomorrow."

CHAPTER EIGHT

December 24th

Ken

The drive to Felicia's farm was nice. A light snow was falling, ensuring that the trees sparkled in the sunshine. While Christmas wasn't his favorite, he'd never minded winter, something Gregory, his mentor and therapist, had spent hours discussing with him.

It wasn't logical that he directed his dislike solely at the commercialized holiday, when the slippery roads were a big part of the car accident that had claimed his parent's lives on Christmas Eve when he'd been only nine-years-old. Still, snow had no intentions, while the woman who'd driven the SUV with reindeer antlers on the windows might have helped his parents had she been intent on helping them. Instead, she'd gotten back into her SUV loaded with Christmas wrapping paper and decorations, taking off from the accident site without even calling for help. She'd been selfish, too scared to be confronted with the consequences of her lack of attention while driving in poor conditions.

WRAPPED UP IN LOVE

That the police had arrested her while exiting her vehicle at a local Christmas market had just been the icing on the proverbial cake. Nothing should get into the way of indulging in the commercial bliss that was Christmas, right? He might have never known about that particularly macabre detail had it not been for a large picture that had ended up in the local newspapers. *Reckless Driver Arrested At Christmas Market*, the headline had read. The subtitle had made his heart constrict: Two lives claimed in car accident, child survives.

It was the kind of thing that could mess with a kid's head, especially one who'd just lost his parents. That everyone had acted strange around him each year around the holidays also hadn't helped, even though he certainly didn't blame his aunt and uncle, nor Johnathan and Felicia, who had just been kids themselves.

Besides his parent's death, for which he bore no responsibility, he only regretted that his own grief had overshadowed the holidays for the rest of his family, so over the years he'd ensured to retreat towards the end of December, ensuring that everyone else could celebrate without feeling like they had to hold back their cheer on his behalf.

It wasn't a sane reaction on an intellectual level, knowing his family would have loved to include him, but it was such an ingrained behavior by now that it came without much effort on his part. His reaction to Tamara and her little tree was enough to reinforce that his self-imposed social exile was the lesser of two evils.

Or maybe it was a sign he needed to re-evaluate his own behavior and feelings.

"It's so beautiful out here," Tamara said, interrupting his morose thoughts, agreeing with his earlier assessment. "I rarely get out of the city and sometimes I forget just how pretty Canada is."

Johnathan laughed. "Just wait until we get to the farm. Felicia and Garret have done a great job of getting it in shape. They bought it, what? Maybe eight years ago now?" He turned to Ken, eyebrows raised in question.

"It was the year before Felicia got pregnant with Mellie, so yeah, it must be eight years now."

"Will your sister be there?" Tamara asked, obviously unsure whether that would be a good thing. Ken almost laughed. The little subbie was smart enough to know that their trip would entail more than a casual stroll through the trees, but she hadn't been able to get anything out of Johnathan or him, though that wasn't for a lack of trying.

She was pleasant to be with. Open-minded, not without humor, and, most importantly, not only beautifully submissive but also self-confident when it came to involving herself in conversations and decision-making processes for things that didn't fall into the kinky parameters of their little auction agreement. Like the way she'd insisted that cereal was the only acceptable breakfast, even though he'd offered to scramble eggs and make some bacon. Apparently, milk and grains were needed to turn a sleepy subbie into a sociable human being in the mornings.

"They'll keep the front booth open until noon today, for all those folks who prefer to set up a freshly cut tree on Christmas Eve, but we won't see them. We'll head to one of the back fields that is closed this year. They always open three sections so people have different sized trees to choose from and the section we're going to is one that is closed to customers this year."

Ken checked the rear-view mirror to watch Tamara's reaction. The way her forehead creased as she tried to decide whether to press Johnathan on *why* they were going to the closed section was adorable.

Johnathan had a thing for primal play, and while Ken was perfectly happy to have his prey nicely delivered in the form of a willing sub, he also couldn't deny the appeal of chasing down his plaything.

As Johnathan steered the car off the highway and down a gravel road, Tamara's attention moved between the outside and inside of the car. Ken could almost hear her brain going from admiring the landscape to "Hold on, you're in the car with two doms who have a plan up their sleeves. Pay attention!" It was the perfect mental preparation for the scene to come, and he enjoyed the heck out of how receptive Tamara was to them.

"Here we go," Johnathan announced as he turned onto an even smaller dirt road, putting the car into park in order to open up a gate.

"Does Felicia know we're going on their property?" Tamara asked from the backseat, sounding bemused.

Ken chuckled. "No, she would have wanted to know why we're going to the closed section and might have even tried to join us for a walk. Neither of those were things we wanted."

Tamara's expression was priceless—a mix of frustration, excitement, and suppressed laughter—and he couldn't help but laugh.

"You doms are evil beings!" Tamara announced, though her smile told him she was still in good spirits about the whole thing.

"Just wait and see," he teased, finding his own adrenaline kicking in with the rising anticipation.

Once Johnathan had pulled through the open gate and parked the car, they got out and Ken nodded for his cousin to explain what was about to happen.

"Okay, since we are outside and in a private location we have some room to explore a bit of the wilder side of play, but for the same reasons, being alone and outside, away from dungeon monitors or other helpers, we'll keep it pretty tame today. Still, it won't be a plain old hike today!" Johnathan said it with a grin that made Tamara blush an adorable shade of pink. "I enjoy a bit of primal play now and again and it was on your list as something you're open to trying, so this should be fun."

Tamara's phone rang suddenly, interrupting them. She looked between them, silently asking whether she should ignore it.

"You better answer it," Ken said. "This should be Master Benjamin's check-in call."

They had planned it so their play would happen between calls, ensuring they wouldn't get interrupted and that Tamara had the chance to raise any concerns if she had them.

"We'll step away," Johnathan said, and they walked a few meters away to give Tamara some space. It wasn't ideal, since it wasn't the best place for Tamara to express concerns, alone in the woods with the two of them, but this wasn't her only check-in call, which gave them a bit more leeway.

After a couple of minutes, Tamara joined them again.

"Thank you for giving me space."

He liked that about her. She was polite and generous with her appreciation, even for little things that shouldn't necessitate any thanks.

He stepped closer to her and ran his hand down her cheek. "You're very welcome, darling."

Unperturbed by the interruption, Johnathan jumped right back into his instructions. "What we're going to do is have you start from here. You'll get a two-minute head start, then we'll chase you."

"You want me to run away from you?" Tamara asked, her voice intrigued rather than appalled.

"Yes, sweetheart. After all, you're a lost reindeer and we're the scary wolves."

Tamara's laughter was full of honest joy. Ken moved closer to her, pulling her back against his front so he could place his hands on her breasts, keeping her in place. There was simply no better way of holding on to a little subbie than by making use of her gorgeous curves, even if they were covered in layers of winter clothing.

His hands slid lower to grab her hips and pull her even tighter, letting her feel his arousal.

Her enthusiasm for various types of play was amazing, and he was all too happy to ensure she got into the proper head-space for the game to come.

Tamara's laughter faded, but he could feel her breathing speed up as his hands traveled up again. Winter coats weren't exactly ideal for fondling, but the mere suggestion of holding her in place like this obviously resonated with her. Pretty little submissive.

Johnathan shot him an amused look. Okay, so maybe he was getting a bit ahead of the plan.

Focusing on Tamara, his cousin laid out the rules they'd come up with. "We'll chase you, and when we catch you, which we inevitably will, of course, you'll be our prey. Since you are a runner and pretty fit, we'll base our rules on that. Let's say that if we catch you within less than ten minutes, we'll undress you right here in the freezing cold forest and mark you as ours. If you escape for longer than that, you'll have to be punished thoroughly for giving us a hard time, but we'll do that in the comfort of Ken's warm house."

"It sounds like the big bad wolves are the ones who'll win either way," Tamara protested, amusement clear in her words.

Johnathan shrugged, while Ken let his hand travel lover until he reached the lower seam of her coat, pushing it up so he could cup her crotch. "You wouldn't want to play a game that leaves wild animals angry, would you?" He growled in her ear, finding himself enjoying this little game Johnathan had come up with.

Maybe he needed to explore his own interests a bit more in the new year. He'd gotten into a stuck set of behaviors in more ways than one, it seemed.

Tamara let her head fall back against his shoulder, exposing her throat the same way an animal who was submitting might. "That does sound like a bad idea when you put it like that. Angry wolves could very well turn into a real problem."

Johnathan, taking advantage of the opportunity, stepped against Tamara's front, leaving her pinned between them. Leaning forward, his cousin kissed Tamara's throat while Ken nipped at her earlobe.

"Then you better run now, little reindeer."

They both stepped away, watching as Tamara's glazed expression took a moment to clear, before she sprinted off into the Christmas trees, giggling.

"Looks like she's into it," Johnathan said, sounding pleased.

"Yup, she's not one to balk at trying something new."

Johnathan gave him a considering look. "Neither are you, apparently."

Ken scoffed. "You've got to give me some credit. I'm not as boring as all that." He purposely neglected to admit that he'd been thinking something rather similar only a moment earlier.

WRAPPED UP IN LOVE

Laughing, Johnathan nodded towards the trees. "Are we really going to give her two minutes?"

"Nah, let's go."

Chapter Nine

December 24th

Tamara

The two men were getting closer, their boots crunching on the fresh snow. Tamara was already sweating under her heavy winter coat, knowing full well that no self-respecting dom would let her get away with half-assing a chase like this.

Adrenaline was pumping through her body as she ran. Before this auction, she had exclusively played in the club. Now, of course, she had played at Ken's house, too, but that was not at all comparable to the thrill of being out here, knowing that when Master Johnathan and Master Ken caught up with her, they'd take her body and make it theirs.

Claim her completely this time.

She kept sprinting when something hit her back.

Turning back to see what it was, her foot caught on the thin ice layer forming on top of the snow. She was falling. Any second, the hard ground would teach her a lesson in paying attention. Fortunately, the snow prevented her from landing on the hard ground directly, though that didn't mean she enjoyed getting more closely acquainted with the white stuff.

What the heck had hit her?

Looking around, she quickly spotted the culprit.

It was a snowball.

As the realization hit, her hands were already reaching out to form one of her own, hurling it towards Master Johnathan, who was beelining towards her between the trees. He was still relatively far away, so her snowball landed on the ground, never making it to her target.

Scrambling up, she jumped between two trees, darting in a new direction. Master Johnathan was closing in on her. Giggles escaped her despite the way the cold air burned in her lungs. She was feeling like a kid again, playing in the snow. Except that she also felt damn hot in a very adult kind of way.

She was wanted.

They both wanted her. Chased her for it.

When she'd written that she was open to try primal play on her form, she hadn't really been able to picture just how exhilarating it would be. Or that it would involve a proper chase scene.

When Johnathan closed in on her left, she veered right, realizing too late that it had been a trap. She'd been so focused on her obvious pursuer that she'd forgotten to listen for Master Ken.

He was right there, one tree to her left. Pushing herself harder and faster, she veered around another tree, using it to put an obstacle between herself and the two doms. Then she bolted, the muscles in her legs burning with the effort.

She made it three strides before hard arms encircled her. Together, they tumbled to the ground, but somehow Master Ken pulled her on top of him, cushioning her fall.

Struggling a little to keep with the game, she used her movements to snuggle in closer to his warm body. His aftershave matched the fresh scent of pine needles all around them. Way better than any of those scented candles she'd bought to mimic a similar smell. Woodsy and sexy as hell. She'd probably never hike in a forest again without thinking about him.

Master Johnathan came to a halt beside them, skidding over the snow on his knees. Clearly, he didn't want to miss out on being included in future daydreams while hiking.

As Master Ken held her upper body and arms encircled on top of him, Johnathan leaned down over her, pressing his cold lips against her own frozen ones. Immediately she felt the heat inside her travel to the place where their bodies met, the kiss deep and demanding.

This wasn't the easy-going Johnathan she was so used to. This was a hunter who'd caught his prey, driven by an instinct that made him want to claim her now.

As their kiss broke, Master Ken released her, but only to allow her to sit up. Then he collected both her hands behind her back, holding them in the grip of one hand, forcing her to bend at the hip by pressing his other hand against her nape.

It was an utterly submissive position and her need soared higher.

Bending forward, she could feel his erection hard against her ass, even through his jeans and her fleece lined pants.

"Got you, little one."

Johnathan

The little subbie was breathing heavily, held down by his cousin.

"We could undress you completely. After all, we caught you in," he checked his watch, "nine minutes and fifty-five seconds. Or you could beg for leniency."

Tamara's chuckle was lower than usual. She was enjoying this as much as they were. "I would not dare deny a wild wolf his feast."

The little minx was challenging him. Laughing, he nodded at Ken, who grinned back at him. This was even more fun than he'd thought it would be.

"Don't mind if I do," he agreed, pulling a condom package from his pocket. When he pulled down Tamara's pants, she gasped.

It was pretty chilly, so they couldn't be long.

As if thinking the same thing, Ken felt Tamara's pussy and, finding it slick with arousal, covered himself with a condom and slid into her. Entering her a few times with deep, slow strokes, he finally nodded at Johnathan.

"You ready for more?" he asked, hoping to all hell she was up for it.

"God, yes." Her moaned response was like a balsam for his soul.

Ken was still holding her hands between her back, giving her some support from falling forward, which left her face at the perfect height.

Opening his pants, he stepped forward and guided his cock toward her face. "Open up, pet."

The heat of her sweet mouth after the painful moment of icy wind was the best feeling in the world.

Watching his cousin's rhythm for a couple of seconds, he began to move, ensuring one of them filled her at all times.

Her moaning against his cock was driving him mad, and he was pretty sure he couldn't hold out long, even if he wanted.

"Best not to let this pretty ass get too cold," Ken said, giving Tamara's behind a little slap that made her nip Johnathan's cock.

"Watch it," he complained, realizing that his usually serious cousin was apparently beyond amused.

"You watch it," Ken replied, intensifying the rhythm of his strokes.

Johnathan didn't argue. Ken was right. They needed to make sure Tamara didn't get too cold. Pulling his cock out of her mouth, he stepped back, though he kept his hands on her shoulders, helping to steady her.

"Here, hang on to the tree." As Ken adjusted his stance, Johnathan directed Tamara to take hold of the exposed stem of a somewhat sparse white pine. Luckily, her gloves and long sleeves meant the needles of the tree wouldn't bother her.

With her securely in place, Ken pounded into her, and Tamara's whines and moans told them she was enjoying every bit of it.

Sheathing himself in a condom, Johnathan tugged his now deflated cock into his pants. Damn, but it was cold.

When Ken came, he held on to Tamara for a moment, before nodding at Johnathan. That seemed enough for his cock to wake up from his hibernation, because he could feel himself hardening again.

Stepping forward, he stroked himself a few times before he was ready. Then he sank into the glorious heat that was the pretty little submissive they'd caught. He didn't reach around to tease Tamara. While he wanted her to enjoy herself, this was about claiming her and they had more plans tonight. Letting her get off now would be nice, but driving her mad with need and then making her wait had an appeal all on its own.

And tonight they'd need her begging.

Her ass was gaining a pink color from the cold, so he quickened his movements, finding himself close to release quickly.

"Clench for me, sweet girl," he ordered, and she complied, her pussy wringing his cock in quick pulses.

"Fuck, you're hot," he praised as he released his cum.

As he used a tissue to clean himself up, tying the condom and letting it disappear in his coat pocket, Ken helped Tamara stand. His cousin kneeled as he pulled up Tamara's pants, beginning the process of providing aftercare.

She looked gorgeous, her eyes wide from excitement, adrenaline, and burning need.

Just the way they wanted her.

"You fucked me against a Christmas tree."

There was an excited wonder in her tone that was all kinds of wrong and made him grin. "Sure did."

"I guess this is one way to pick the right tree." Tamara's voice was lilting slightly and Johnathan was surprised to find that their little game had pushed her further into the headspace than he'd expected.

He stepped closer, wrapping an arm around her. "You like the tree?"

Tamara just nodded, her eyes still wide, now looking at the tree she'd clung to just moments earlier.

Johnathan raised his eyebrows at his cousin.

After a moment, Ken agreed. "We can take the tree."

Johnathan waited a few heartbeats, watching Ken's expression and body language, but his cousin truly showed no aversion to the idea.

Now that was new.

Maybe it had something to do with the image of Tamara hanging on to the pine as they'd taken her. Johnathan could honestly say that as far as he was concerned, that visual was definitely going to stay with him for quite a while. There was really no way Ken hadn't cataloged that particular experience for future reference.

While Ken settled Tamara into the truck with a blanket, Johnathan went to the back of his truck where he kept the saw he used to cut up thick branches for his training with the dogs.

Would be a shame not to have a fresh tree on Christmas morning.

CHAPTER TEN

December 24th

Tamara

Master Ken's bathroom was perfect. Standing in the shower, which was about three times as big as the tiny one she had at home, the hot water ran over her, warming up those places the hot chocolate hadn't been able to warm. They had blasted the heat in the truck on the way home and shared hot chocolate from a thermos, but there was nothing better than a steamy shower to chase away the remnants of the cold that had seeped through her wet clothes on the drive home.

Reluctantly, she turned off the water and stepped out of the shower, a fresh wave of energy rushing through her. By all that was right, she should be exhausted, but the thought of going to the club with not only one, but two doms was too thrilling to allow anything resembling exhaustion to take hold.

In her temporary bedroom, she looked over at her Christmas tree and smiled. It was no longer the only tree she would enjoy this year. Master Ken may not love

Christmas, but despite his initial grumpiness, he was trying not to dampen her own excitement for the holidays. And wasn't that just sweet?

With that in mind, she picked the outfit she'd been least sure about when packing. It was a cupless corset in a soft blue fabric that had a satin finish. The top tied to the G-string panties with delicate bows, and the entire fabric was sheer. She'd found it on sale last month when shopping with Casey and had bought it mostly because she liked the idea of being someone who could feel confident wearing something so overtly seductive. At the same time, she hadn't been sure she would actually work up the courage to put it on.

Determined to please Master Ken after he'd given in to having her decorate an actual tree in his house, she pulled on the lingerie and paired it with a white tulle skirt, checking herself in the mirror on the back of the door.

Her cheeks looked rosy, either from the shower or the drastically increased amount of non-self-administered orgasms. Her hair was shiny from the product she'd used and her make-up looked decent, which was probably because she used as little as possible. Any use of heavy eyeliner or the like always led to her looking like a thirteen-year-old who was starting on an early teenage emo phase. Make-up so wasn't her thing.

Good enough.

Pulling on a pair of tights and her trench coat, she headed downstairs to where the two Masters were already waiting. Both of them studied her as she got closer, and the amount of masculine attention was doing funny things to her.

How did Casey do it, being married to a man who always looked at her like that? It was definitely doing funny things to her own libido, and certainly didn't hurt her self-confidence.

All through the car ride, the silky material she was wearing moved against her skin and the mix of nervousness and excitement made her twitchy. It took some serious effort to keep her hands still.

Being the doms they were, both Master Ken and Master Johnathan definitely noticed, their eyes continuously raking over her coat and tights. She could almost hear their brains trying to figure out what she was wearing underneath.

Hopefully, they would like it.

She didn't really know what their preferences were. Club B wasn't a huge club in terms of membership, but she usually played with the same people. It wasn't that she was particularly interested in any one of them, though she certainly like all of her regular play partners, but it was part of her safety strategy. She was an outgoing person, and loved meeting new people, but she'd had to learn that giving your trust away too easily could end up badly, so when she'd entered the lifestyle, she'd set a set of rules for herself that she followed. This auction was her giving herself leave to follow her personality and live a little more.

Her life had become stale in the past years, and it was time to make some changes. Her come-to-heart talk with Casey about what she wanted out of life and whether she didn't want a family one day had been a bit of a wake-up call. Watching her friend get married and now start on having a family was amazing, but it had also highlighted how her own self-reliance had slowly turned into a form of unconscious loneliness.

It was time to make changes, but first, she'd treat herself to something wild. And heck if it wasn't already worth it.

She met Master Johnathan's eyes as he looked over at her again. He'd chosen to sit next to her in the car's rear, and his proximity did funny things to her stomach.

Johnathan

The little subbie was more fidgety than a trout on a hook, and the way she kept running her hands down her coat was a dead giveaway she was wearing something special for their trip to the club.

His dick gave a little nudge as they drove up the club's driveway. Luckily, the cold meant there was no lingering around outside, and they all walked into the club's small lobby with quick steps. After showing their membership cards to Johnathan, Tamara headed into the women's locker room, while he and Ken dropped their own coats in the men's room.

"So what do you think she's got on under that coat?" Ken asked, bemused.

"She was definitely nervous about showing it off, so it's bound to be good."

Ken's smile was that of a little boy in a candy store. It wasn't an expression Johnathan saw often on his cousin and he was damn glad he'd pitched in on the auction. For more than one reason.

"Let's check if our room is ready."

"I'll go. You wait for Tamara." Entering the main club room, Ken walked off, leaving Johnathan to check the crowd.

It wasn't busy today, most people preferring to spend a quiet Christmas Eve with family, but some regulars were there. While Johnathan usually enjoyed mingling and loved the energy of the busier Saturday nights, he couldn't find the motivation to walk over to join any of the conversations. Instead, he leaned against the back of a booth. From here, he had a good view of the women's locker room door.

"Tamara about to come out?" a teasing voice asked from behind him.

Turning, he saw Jessica and Master Benjamin in the booth behind him. Both of them were smiling at him, though Benjamin tucked on his sub's hair in admonishment for her nosiness.

Johnathan felt his lips tug upward. "Yup, and I'm pretty sure she's debuting some fancy outfit."

Benjamin chuckled. "Nervous, was she?"

Johnathan nodded, the picture of Tamara in the car making his smile grow wider.

"You liked the auction then?" Jessica asked, obviously back in her role as club owner, checking whether the events she was putting on worked for her members.

"Yeah, things worked out rather well."

He would have kept talking with the two, but at that moment, the door to the women's locker room opened and Tamara walked out. Her blond waves framed her face and trailed down over her shoulder, leading right to her gorgeous breasts.

Which were bare.

"Oh, fuck me." He couldn't hold back the moan and didn't give a shit about it.

Tamara looked like a wet dream come to life. He'd expected her to wear something nice, but the sheer skirt that showed just the hint of the blue triangle over her pussy matched with the corset that left her perky breasts peeking out was about the hottest damn thing he'd ever seen. And he'd seen some fucking nice lingerie in the club.

"Better fetch your sub before someone else tries their luck," Benjamin said, laughing as Johnathan pushed off the booth and headed for Tamara. It may have been a joke, but he was damned if he didn't get possessive at the thought of another man approaching Tamara.

The closer he got, the more of her creamy skin he could see. He had no clue why some women got so nervous about wearing clothes designed to arouse men, because from where he stood he'd never *not* liked to see a woman in lingerie. Nothing had prepared him to see Tamara like this, though.

"You're hot as hell, woman," he said, once he got close enough.

Her large blue eyes looked up at him with a twinkle of excitement. "Thanks?" It came out sounding like a question, so he pulled her against him, pressing his mouth over hers. Using his tongue to tease her lips until she opened up for him, he made sure she had no more doubts about how hot she looked.

When he finally released her, Tamara's cheeks looked rosy in that kissed mindless kind of way and suddenly Johnathan wanted to get her into the private room as soon as possible. Whether it was that strange new possessiveness that drove him to get her away from everyone else, or his dick demanding he keep touching her, he couldn't quite tell, but when he took her hand, she smiled up at him with desire burning in her eyes.

Obviously, she didn't mind his eagerness.

The theme rooms offered a variety of experiences, but while they each had a certain appeal, they had decided on a very specific one that would serve their purposes well. The decor was that of a tropical resort and the back wall was painted to resemble the look out onto a sandy beach, palm trees, glistening water, and all. The other walls made it look as if they were inside a fancy suite, looking out through open balcony doors.

While the painted walls provided the setting, the actual room was fairly sparse in its furnishings, since one piece of equipment dominated the room. A large swing hung from the ceiling in the center, providing excellent access to whomever was sitting in it.

And access was exactly what they wanted.

"Well, fuck me," Ken said, his usual aversion to cursing forgotten when he saw Tamara.

Johnathan had to grin. "That's pretty much exactly what I said when I saw her."

Tamara's smile grew. "I suppose it's good we're in the club, then."

Laughing, he tugged her further into the room to close the door behind her. He loved her easy going, adventurous nature. In fact, they were extremely well-matched in personality and kinks, which was something he hadn't expected when he'd backed Ken's bid. While he enjoyed playing with a variety of partners, he hadn't come across someone so easy and yet exciting to be with.

"Come here," Ken told Tamara, and Johnathan stepped out of the way to allow his cousin to pull her into his arms, kissing her in the same way he had only minutes earlier. Somehow, he felt none of the possessiveness he had battled at the thought of anyone else touching her. Then again, Ken and he had grown up as siblings after his aunt and uncle had died, so they were used to sharing their things.

Their woman.

It had a nice ring to it.

And they were about to take things all the way tonight.

He approached the two of them, both still entwined in their kiss. Ken, noticing his approach, looked at him and broke off the kiss, though he held Tamara encircled in his arms. Nodding, Ken signaled him to step up behind her, which was exactly what he'd intended.

The sheer skirt she was wearing wasn't much of a barrier, so when he pressed his body against hers, his cock fit snuggly into the perfect groove between her ass cheeks. It felt like she was made to welcome him there, and wouldn't it be almost rude to ignore such a sweet invitation?

CHAPTER ELEVEN

December 24th

Tamara

Her heart was hammering inside her very exposed chest. The two of them had her trapped between them, pressing their lengths against her in a way that didn't leave a glimmer of doubt that her choice of lingerie had the desired effect.

They wanted her.

And it looked like they wanted her on that large swing that hung from the ceiling in the middle of the room. It was one thing she'd never tried. Well, it was one of two things she'd never tried.

Double penetration was the other.

And yet, engulfed in the safety of Master Ken's and Master Johnathan's arms, she didn't feel nervous. Not anymore. It was as if she'd exhausted her nervousness on the drive over. Now she was excited. Maybe even eager.

The way Master Johnathan nibbled on her ear was distracting enough that she almost didn't notice when

Master Ken gripped her skirt, tearing it apart with one hard jerk of his hands.

"What are you doing?"

"It was in my way. I'll pay for a replacement, of course."

She stared at him in disbelief. "I don't care about the money."

He looked back at her with his calm, measured gaze. Unyielding. "Then what are you worried about? Surely you didn't think you'd be keeping it on?"

Words were evading her, so she just opened her mouth without the smart reply that surely would come to her later.

Unperturbed by her reaction, Ken tilted his head and looked at Johnathan. "Although, I figure we should have her keep on that corset. I'm rather fond of it."

In response, Johnathan's hands moved around her to play with her exposed nipples. "Oh yes, this should definitely stay on."

When her arms moved up, Ken shook his head. "No, Tamara. You're ours to play with. You won't cover yourself."

Her hands sank to her sides as if he'd somehow taken over control of her body. And in a way, he had.

They had.

Johnathan's hands let go of her breasts and, instead, took her shoulders to push her towards the swing. "Time to make you fly, sweetheart."

WRAPPED UP IN LOVE

The soft pieces of faux fur Master Ken had wrapped around the various pieces of the swing ensured that none of the nylon straps pressed into her uncomfortably. Sitting upright, her weight rested on a thin strap under her ass and loops around her knees. There was also a strap behind her lower back to keep her from falling backwards.

It was typical that the two men had thought to bring something to make things more comfortable for her. They were as caring as Andrew was with Casey, and wasn't that a strange thought?

It was probably a dom thing. Control and caring, the two principal characteristics of a good lifestyle dominant.

Despite the added comfort, her position was disconcertingly vulnerable. Above her, an adjustable bar connected to her knee restraints, and Master Johnathan hadn't hesitated to use it, spreading her legs wide. It left her pussy open for their inspection. And more.

They hadn't pulled her legs so wide apart that it would get painful over time, but Tamara was pretty sure that when they let her back down, her legs would take a while before feeling normal again. Even without all the things they were planning on doing to her.

Master Johnathan took a seat on the chair he'd placed in front of her, grinning up at her for only seconds before he moved his face closer and started licking her core. Her nerve endings exploded with the soft touch of his skilled tongue. Her inability to move away when he increased his pressure made her feel even more submissive. There was no great way of describing the mindset of utterly losing control. Except maybe blissful. All she could do was feel as his tongue glided and flicked over her.

He wasn't rough on her clit like some of the more inexperienced men she'd been with. No, he knew how to tease around and around, as skilled as Master Ken had been. In between sucking on her clit in a rhythmic pattern, he was only giving her the gentlest of touches that were driving her crazy. Leaving her wanting to beg for more.

And she did. She begged, driven to desperation by the need he was creating. Johnathan didn't move, only chuckled. The warm breaths of air escaping his lips traveled to her core, almost as seductive as the movements of his tongue.

Behind her, there was the rustling of clothes, and then Master Ken stepped against her back.

A promise of more.

His hands slit around her waist until they met on her stomach, enveloping her. Moving up until he cupped her breasts, he used his fingers to pinch and twist her nipples, creating delicious waves of pain that ripples through her.

Her core filled with desire coursing through her, making her sink deeper into the swing. Or maybe it was only her mind that gave way, not her body. She was weightless. Nothing was pressing down on her except desire and need. And they were fueling it, feeding it, making her theirs.

"She's already nice and puffy," Master Johnathan said, sounding pleased.

In her fuzzy mind, she noted his words made her feel good, like she'd done something right, even though she hadn't moved at all. Couldn't move.

Hm, how nice this was.

"I love how responsive you are, Tamara." Master Ken's voice was a murmured praise.

Johnathan rose from his chair, and the two men stepped away from her. Losing their proximity made wariness encroach on her bliss.

"We're just getting set for you, sweetheart," Master Johnathan reassured her, running a hand over her thigh.

It wasn't enough. He didn't reach the place where she really needed him.

She grumbled, not bothering with actual words. They would know what she meant.

"We won't take our eyes off of you," Master Ken said. Ignoring her whining, his tone was matter of fact. "You look gorgeous like that, all spread for us. We'll make sure you're safe. We'll make sure you'll feel good."

Coming from him, the words rang true. Because they would make sure she'd feel good. They'd already proved to her they could. And something inside of her told her she could trust them. Trust them to keep her safe.

She nodded, and Master Ken's gaze softened. "Brave girl."

They both pulled off their pants and rolled condoms over their erect shafts. Then Master Johnathan took a large bottle of lube and covered himself before handing it over to Master Ken, who did the same, generously, before putting the bottle on the sideboard.

"The lube will be within my reach in case I need more."

Because he'd take her ass now.

She'd done anal play before, plenty of times, in fact. And she'd enjoyed it, too, even though it had the strange effect of making her feel extra naughty.

When you regularly visited a bondage club, you might think all the play would lose its taboo feeling eventually—or at least she had thought so in the beginning—, but there were always certain things that made you feel like you were doing something particularly wicked. And yet, the prospect of not one but two cocks entering her at once was definitely putting her body on high alert in a very good way.

Even in her drowsy mind, she knew she could have backed out otherwise, with no one blaming her for even a second.

She wouldn't, though.

As if in response to her inner determination, Master Johnathan stepped between her legs. Immediately, her pussy ached for his touch, but her focus split when Master Ken positioned himself behind her. The dazed feeling that had clouded her thoughts while Johnathan had driven her close to orgasm earlier had faded into non-existence.

She was hyper aware of them now, trying to predict their every movement.

"Relax, sweetheart." Master Johnathan stepped even closer, running his hands up her legs on either side, pushing the swing back until she was flush against Master Ken's chest.

Her position kept her pelvis from tilting forward too much, allowing Master Johnathan ample access to her pussy, while also making it easy for Master Ken to access her ass. Because that was what Master Ken had positioned himself for, running his hands down her back in a tantalizing path toward the place he intended to invade.

"Stop thinking." This time Master Johnathan's voice was stern, and her eyes met his in a subconscious desire to please him. He still had his laugh lines, but he was watching her carefully now. "Let us do the work. You just need to relax."

She nodded, but he shook his head and chuckled. "I see you'll need a bit more convincing."

He closed the remaining distance between them, his lubed up cock hitting against her pussy as he moved in on her. She truly was at the perfect height for him.

Even as her nerves were firing excited bursts of arousal to her brain, Master Johnathan captured her mouth in a deep kiss, driving any thought out of her mind. And then he entered her.

Her body responded with eagerness, her pussy constricting around him, still seeking the release they had denied her at the tree farm. She wanted more, but Master Johnathan's movements were slow, almost lazy, a maddening contrast to his upbeat personality.

"Please," she begged, and she wasn't sure whether she wanted Johnathan to move faster or Master Ken to finally move and help get her closer to that point of release that she wanted so desperately.

The swing might have moved back from the pressure of Master Johnathan's body moving against hers, if it hadn't been for his cousin who was standing behind her, wrapping his arms around her, holding her in place. Master Ken's hands didn't roam, didn't tease, instead he simply held her against him, as his cousin claimed her body.

Master Johnathan went slowly at first. As his cock moved in and out of her, her eyes closed. The sensation of him moving inside of her was everything she'd been craving for the past two days.

Being with the two Masters had turned her body into a wanton thing. Needing more and more. And now she was getting more, and it felt damn good.

Just as she was sinking into the bliss of the same sensation repeating over and over, Master Ken's hands moved down her body, first touching her breasts, then sinking even lower yet, his fingers dipping between her spread folds. Whether it was her own slickness or the remaining lube on his fingers, he slid over her clit easily, gently coaxing her to that place where she no longer worried and simply desired.

A whine escaped her.

Everything they did was perfect, and yet it wasn't enough.

It didn't matter. They were doing what they wanted, and no begging would make them change their plans.

The knowledge made the tension she'd held onto morph into molten lava inside of her.

Need.

"Your turn," Master Johnathan said in a gruff voice, and Tamara saw through half-lidded eyes how he nodded at Master Ken behind her.

He stopped massaging her clit and a moment later she felt him nudge her ass.

Master Johnathan was now holding her waist, ensuring she stayed in place, while Master Ken's hands spread her ass cheeks to position himself, the tip of his cock pressing against her first softly, then with an ever-growing pressure.

"You're doing amazing, sweetheart," Johnathan murmured, nuzzling her neck and covering her with distracting kisses.

"You can use your safe word or yellow whenever you need," Ken added, as he continued to press against her.

She wasn't afraid, knowing the discomfort would only be momentary and ease with the wanton arousal that anal penetration could bring. So she pressed down on Master Ken as best as she could in her position.

It took less than two seconds and the head of his cock had pressed past the barrier of her muscle, causing the overwhelming stretching sensation to take her breath away for a moment. Usually she'd been on her knees when having anal sex in the past, and this felt different.

She had less control. Couldn't move away if she didn't like something, or if the pressure grew too much.

Her heart hammered, and her mind grew fuzzy.

Only now did she realize that Master Johnathan had pulled himself completely out of her, leaving her empty. Despite the internal turmoil his retreat was causing her, he waited patiently as his cousin slowly but surely moved in and out of her, pressing forward until, eventually, Master Ken filled her completely, his balls snug against her ass. He stopped for a beat, before pulling back and repeating the move a few times while Master Johnathan massaged her breasts, her nipples hard peaks under his hands.

"Ready," Master Ken said, and Master Johnathan gave her an approving smile.

"You're doing amazing, Tamara," Master Ken murmured into her ear, his front pressed against her back, warming her. The words hummed through her, making her feel good.

With some sort of communication, Master Ken pulled almost all the way out, before Master Johnathan pressed back into her. The moan that escaped her was so animistic, it almost startled her.

"Yes, baby, you're taking us like a very good girl," Master Ken praised, before pushing back in.

They found a rhythm, one in, the other out, and all she could do was feel.

There was nothing else than the stretching and stroking of her most sensitive spots, and then suddenly there was more. Master Johnathan's hands on her breasts. Master Ken's fingers finding her clit again, circling and teasing her. It was driving her mad and sounds broke from her in a way she'd never experienced before. Whining, screaming, begging, and moaning. She couldn't feel embarrassed, too far gone in the sensations they were gifting her.

She was getting closer and closer like a volcano about to erupt. She needed it, the pressure growing with a force that grew overwhelming.

"I need to come. Oh god. Please." No more coherent words would come, so she just moaned her desperate need.

"You've been such a good girl," Master Johnathan murmured, his own voice strained. "On three."

He counted down and her body tensed for only a second. Then Master Ken pinched her clit and Johnathan twisted her nipples as both their cocks pressed into her at the same time.

Everything went black as the most intense orgasm of her life shook through her body, removing her from all feelings except for the ripples that shook through her, leaving her completely bare to the two men that had purchased her at the auction.

Chapter Twelve

December 25th

Ken

Waking up, the first thing he noticed was the lack of another body. No warm curves where a soft woman should be curled up next to him.

They'd all fallen asleep in his king-sized bed together, Tamara in the middle, since neither Johnathan nor he had wanted to miss out on holding Tamara after the way she'd allowed them to claim her so beautifully last night.

The next thing that drew his attention was the smell. It differed from the way his house usually smelled. Not the normal scent of his cleaner. Instead, it smelled like someone was cooking or maybe baking already.

He must have slept longer than he usually did.

No surprise really, since yesterday had been an emotional day, despite the effective way in which Johnathan and Tamara had distracted him.

Stretching, he got up and made his way over to take a shower. He'd showered last night, but there was really no other way to truly wake up in the mornings.

Yesterday was probably the first year that he had truly enjoyed Christmas Eve since he was eight-years-old. Sure, he'd thought of his parents, but it hadn't consumed his thoughts. It was definite progress and Gregory would be pleased to hear it when he would call later on to check in on his friend and patient.

Smiling to himself, he remembered how Tamara had come downstairs, carrying a few Christmas ornaments she must have pulled from her little tree right after they'd returned from their trip to the Christmas Tree Farm. Still in her wet clothes, she'd quietly opened the screen doors that led to his backyard deck where Johnathan had deposited the tree upon their arrival. She hadn't noticed him standing in the kitchen, where he'd watched as she hung them on the tree with the excitement of a little girl.

It hadn't been about the commercial appeal of ornaments and showing off some idyllic image people liked to post on social media. The ornaments were cheap and the tree rather shabby, and yet it had brought her joy. And if he wasn't mistaken, she'd simply wanted to share it with someone.

He hadn't been able but to smile at her enthusiasm. Not for a second had he thought that she'd meant to do something that might upset him. She'd simply been taken in by the excitement she associated with the holidays, and that was sweet in its own way.

Nobody had suggested bringing the tree inside, undoubtedly to respect his preferences. But it was still easily visible through the large window in his living room, and the way Tamara's eyes had sparkled and the way Johnathan had smiled, had reminded him of the positive side of the holiday. The reason he'd withdrawn from his family in the past years. He hadn't been ready to be happy, and he'd hated the idea of taking any joy away from the people he loved.

But by being alone, he'd indulged in his bad attitude and overlooked the good parts of Christmas.

Those ornaments hadn't been about a commercialized celebration for Tamara. She'd picked a few old ornaments off of her own tree to share them with him and Johnathan. Or maybe she pulled them out because they brought her joy during a time of year when she was usually alone.

He'd been a grump and had held her back from something she really enjoyed, and he had no good reason for it other than his misguided grudge. He dried himself off and pulled on some sweats. Today, he would make more of an effort to give Tamara the things that brought her happiness.

She deserved it.

Walking downstairs, the smells he'd woken up to intensified. Cinnamon, vanilla, and something citrusy. Orange probably. He could hear the chatter of Tamara and Johnathan, and the homey atmosphere was surprisingly appealing.

"Good morning," he greeted as he stepped into the kitchen. Both of them turned and Tamara gave him a hesitant smile, whereas Johnathan looked at him without the usual grin on his face. Instead, his cousin looked almost hesitant, too.

"I decided to bake. I hope that's okay?" Tamara asked, her eyes flitting over to Johnathan as if hoping for his help.

Well, damn. Had he really come across as such a tyrant on their first day together that she was this worried about baking something? He'd figured since then they'd gotten along rather well. Especially given all the orgasms they'd both had.

Perhaps Johnathan had shared about his past and now she felt awkward. It wasn't like there was some rule against talking about his parent's passing, and the loss had been his cousin's too, even if it hadn't been quite as difficult for Johnathan as it had been for Ken himself.

Apparently, it was time to reassure the little subbie.

"No, you're perfectly welcome to use the kitchen. What are you making?" An inkling already told him what it was.

"Cookies?" she said, making it sound like a question.

He breathed in deeply, trying to ignore the way his cousin's eyes were analyzing his every move.

"I like cookies." It wasn't the most insightful thing to say, but he figured it was still good enough because Tamara's smile grew.

"Oh, that's good. I also pressed some fresh orange juice for you both."

Now his eyebrows shot up. "You did, did you?"

Tamara gestured towards the table where a tall glass of freshly pressed orange juice was waiting for him.

Walking over, he sat down and took a sip. "This is good." It also explained the citrusy scent.

It had been a long time since he'd had freshly pressed juice, and he'd forgotten just how much better it tasted. The tangy flavor was slightly sour, the perfect thing first thing in the morning. "You'll spoil me for the bought stuff."

Johnathan chuckled. "Yeah, I could get used to this, too."

Tamara's melodic laughter was a wonderful sound. "Well, I don't think I would do it every day, but after last night, I kind of wanted to do something…" She let her sentence trail off, as if she wasn't sure how to express what she meant.

"Last night, eh?" Johnathan teased. "Why don't you tell us more about what you thought was so good about last night?"

Now Tamara full-on laughed. "You're fishing for compliments."

Ken found himself laughing, too. "He's needy like that."

Johnathan's kick against his shin was going to leave a bruise. "Maybe I just wanted her to reassure you. We wouldn't want you thinking that you pale in comparison to me."

Tamara was grinning hard when she met his eyes.

"And what do you say to that?" he challenged her, making her giggle.

"Neither one of you has anything to worry about in that regard, but I think my body might need a little break this morning after all the things we did yesterday."

A contented feeling spread through Ken. They really had gone all out yesterday and he didn't mind slowing things down today. He enjoyed Tamara's company. She was like Johnathan in many ways. Easy to be with, fun and outgoing. As someone who was more of an introvert, he enjoyed her company immensely, especially since he could lean back and enjoy his cousin's and her conversation during breakfast while leaning back and eating his food.

Occasionally, Johnathan would look over at him, as if checking if he was still holding things together, which was putting a slight damper on his mood, but he did his best to ignore it. For now, he'd avoided the melancholy of the day, and he didn't need his cousin's overbearing concern reminding him of what day it was.

Tamara was his perfect distraction, and he intended to allow her to do just that. She was step one in his effort to turn over a new leaf and work on his issues in the same way he recommended to his patients. One step at a time.

This year, he'd try to embrace company and distraction.

Lots of sexy distraction.

Tamara

"Let's head on over to the living room." Master Ken looked like he was determined to suppress his own reluctance.

He'd seemed fine all throughout breakfast and hadn't even bulked at the Christmas cookies that were currently cooling on the stove-top. Knowing his aversion to Christmas, she'd made plain round cookies, instead of star or Christmas tree shaped ones. They'd taste the same, and this way, she hoped, it would ease Master Ken's discomfort.

The better she got to know him, the more she was certain he had a good reason for his dislike of all things Christmas.

But a holiday without cookies was unthinkable, and it wasn't like cookies didn't exist during the rest of the year. So, she'd gone ahead and baked them, and Master Ken had seemed fine with it.

Now, though, he seemed to grow a little more antsy.

She had pulled on a simple green shift dress, but had skipped her usual red Christmas socks with Rudolph on them in favor of knee high black socks that were incredibly fluffy, making her feel like she was walking on clouds.

In the living room, she peeked at the Christmas tree standing outside. With the handful of Christmas ornaments on the large tree, it should have looked ridiculous, but the tiny, almost hidden reminders that it was Christmas made her feel giddy with excitement.

"Since it is Christmas morning, and you agreed to spend the holiday with us," Master Ken started once she'd sat down on the couch, her legs pulled up underneath her, "we wanted to get you a gift. Well, really, it was Johnathan's idea." He looked rueful at that last part, but Johnathan was having none of it.

"Yup, my idea, but Ken came up with what we should get you, so it's a 50/50 effort."

Tamara couldn't hide her smile. The two men, as different as they were, really were like brothers. Teasing but fiercely loyal to each other.

What would it be like to be part of that family? To be protected and cared for by both of these men? To help them in turn?

Master Ken picked up an envelope with a red bow on top. Taking it, she gently opened the flap and pulled out a printed piece of paper with a credit card sized plastic card stuck to it. The face of a shark, it's teeth showing, looked up at her. In red, above the shark, written on the faint blue of the water, were the words *Annual Pass Membership.* Below was the logo of the Toronto aquarium.

"You mentioned you like going there." Master Ken said, and she could hear the smile in his voice. Looked like giving her a Christmas gift hadn't been the cause for his shifting mood. That was a relief.

Looking up, she met first Master Ken's then Master Johnathan's eyes. "This is incredible, but you must have spent a lot of money on this."

Master Johnathan laughed. "Did no one teach you not to ask how much someone spent on your gifts?"

Appalled, she stared at him. "I didn't ask that."

"Good," Master Johnathan said, grinning.

Looking over at Master Ken, who looked perfectly at ease now and simply grinned in a way that suddenly made the family connection between them very apparent, she sighed and looked back down. She knew her smile was growing into a wide grin of her own as she pictured herself visiting the aquarium as often as she could, no longer having to limit her excursions there to the occasional visit.

"Thank you." She hoped they could hear how much the present meant to her, but just to be safe, she got up and kissed each of them. Master Ken's kiss was firm and demanding. Master Johnathan's was teasing and lingering. Both of them were perfect.

As they discussed why she enjoyed visiting the aquarium so much, something she wasn't used to stirred inside of her. It was akin to feeling at home. Not just contentment though, but a peace she'd not felt before.

She was genuinely happy.

Usually, Christmas was a time when she felt proud of herself for what she'd accomplished in her life. She'd built a happy life and landed a successful job despite having been passed around in foster care throughout her youth. There were good foster homes out there, and she was grateful that she'd finally been taken in by two amazing people who'd shown her the value of traditions. They were the ones who had taught her that making an effort to turn your home into something special on Christmas wasn't wasted time. It was time spent making yourself happy, and that counted for something.

This year she'd certainly given herself an exciting Christmas, and right about now, she had absolutely no regrets.

Usually, the pre-Christmas time was when she indulged in her love for the cheesy events that came with the season, but the actual Christmas days were more reflective than outgoing. Eating tons of Christmas cookies and watching movies couldn't compare to actually sharing Christmas morning with two people who were obviously trying to ensure she felt happy.

This year, just for today and tomorrow, she could pretend that she had even more than what she'd worked to gain for herself. She had two men who spoiled her, and she was ready to spoil them right back.

And she could think of a perfect way to do just that.

Chapter Thirteen

December 25th

Johnathan

Just as he was putting the last lunch plate in Ken's dishwasher, the doorbell rang, and Johnathan had a pretty good idea who was going to be outside. Felicia had not been impressed when she'd heard that the one year Ken wasn't holing himself up on Christmas, she hadn't received an invitation. Instead, it had been him their cousin wanted to spend time with.

If she knew the reason for his being here, Johnathan doubted she'd shown up unannounced.

Sisters. They never ceased to show up at inopportune times.

"I'll get it."

Ignoring Ken's expression–a mix of surprise, resignation and frustration–he headed towards the front door. Despite a slight dip in his cousin's mood at the end of breakfast, this was the first actual sign of Ken feeling uncomfortable today, and Johnathan was going to tell his sister off for it. Except, when he opened the door, it wasn't just Felicia standing there. Instead, his younger sister had shown up with her husband and his two nieces in tow.

He should have expected that. It was Christmas, after all.

"Uncle Johnathan," the girls called, jumping into his arms. "Merry Christmas. Merry Christmas. Merry Christmas."

"Merry Christmas to you, too. And to you," he said, wrapping his sister in a hug. She might be a nuisance sometimes, but she was still his nuisance.

After shaking hands with Garret, he stepped back, allowing all of them into the house. Mellie and Cora immediately dropped their shoes in the middle of the hallway, darting into the living room where they expected their other uncle to be.

Johnathan heard a noise that resembled an *uff* sound, telling him they had found their target and had probably jumped into his arms at full speed. He turned the corner himself, seeing his two nieces wrapped around his cousin. Ken was smiling at the girls, but Johnathan could see tension lines forming on his forehead.

Yeah, the morning had gone well, but this might be pushing their luck.

"What are you doing here?" he asked Felicia silently, but she just gave him a stubborn look that told him exactly what she thought of that question.

"What do you think I'm doing? I'm seeing my family on Christmas."

"We have our party tomorrow," he reminded her of the obvious.

"Yes, and Ken never shows up for it. Nor does he usually see anyone on Christmas. So now that he's finally willing to see people, why would I stay away? He is my family just as much as he is yours."

Johnathan sighed. There was no arguing with his sister when she got this stubborn. He met Garret's gaze. His brother-in-law shrugged apologetically. Obviously, he'd tried his luck at keeping Felicia from invading Ken's house but had been unsuccessful.

Felicia strode past him, heading towards Ken, when Mellie and Cora finally noticed Tamara sitting on the couch.

"Who are you?" asked Cora.

"Yeah, who are you?" repeated Mellie.

Felicia stopped in her tracks and stared at Tamara as if she were an alien brought down from space. "Oh, hello. I'm sorry, we didn't know Ken had a guest over."

"You obviously knew I was here," Johnathan argued, trying to get some of the attention off of Tamara, who was looking a little frazzled.

Felicia ignored him, striding up towards Tamara, holding her hand out. "Hi, I'm Felicia. Johnathan's sister and Ken's cousin."

Tamara took her hand and rose. "Hi, it's nice to meet you, Felicia. I've heard a lot about you. I'm Tamara."

"Heard a lot about me?" Felicia looked over at Ken. "Well, that's nice."

She moved across the room to embrace him. "Merry Christmas."

"Merry Christmas," Ken said, sounding somewhat reluctant.

It was time to intervene.

"I have a feeling Mellie and Cora would love some hot chocolate. Ken, why don't you get those ready? Felicia, Garret, do you want some, too?"

His nieces were yelling their excitement. They had undoubtedly spent all morning eating sugary Christmas cookies.

"You should help him," Tamara suggested, clueing in to what he was doing.

Any other time, she would have suggested to go help herself, that much Johnathan was sure of, but she probably thought he had a better shot at figuring out what Ken needed from them.

He nodded at her appreciatively.

With no comment, Ken headed to the kitchen and Johnathan followed suit, feeling only a twinge of guilt for leaving Tamara to preoccupy his sister.

Ken was already pulling mugs out of the cupboard, looking exhausted.

"Are you good with this?" It would be hard to kick Felicia out, but if he made it clear Ken was truly uncomfortable, his sister would put her own hurt aside and leave. Anything to ensure Ken was okay.

"Yeah, it's fine." Ken said. Pouring milk into a pot, he nodded toward the cupboard where he kept the hot chocolate mix. "Get the mix, will you?"

"Felicia knew I would be here today. It's the first year you let anyone come on Christmas, and I think she wanted to bring the girls to cheer you up." It was like his sister to use her adorable girls, whom she knew Ken was absolutely besotted with, to bring some happiness to their cousin. Nuisance or not, she was a great person.

Ken nodded. "Yeah, that was my guess."

Johnathan leaned against the kitchen counter, watching Ken stir the hot chocolate on the stove. "Why is it you never let us visit on Christmas? I mean, I get it. It's a time when you grieve for your parents, but why shut us out?" It was something he'd long wanted to know, but he'd hoped

Ken would share whenever he was ready. Now, though, the time had come to push for an answer.

Ken turned around, looking surprised, despite his best efforts to hide his feelings. They might have to have a conversation about open communication soon, too. As doms they both knew how important it was to be open about their feelings, but then it was a lot easier to push submissives who wanted to be pushed then a dom who'd made it a habit to keep Johnathan out of that particular place of his mind. Even if they were almost brothers.

"I'm not shutting you out. I just don't want to ruin the festivities. Every year, people started walking on eggshells around me. It ruined the holidays. That hardly seemed fair, especially since I know I can be a bit of a Grinch with all the decorations and that stuff."

"Why is that, anyway? Because it reminds you of them?"

Ken shook his head. "No, it reminds me of the greed and irresponsibility of people this time of year, and that usually does a great deal to piss me off."

Johnathan nodded, finally getting it. The woman who'd driven the other vehicle in the car accident had been drinking and had visited some Christmas market after the accident instead of staying to provide first aid or help. It made sense and he couldn't believe he hadn't put it together until now, always figuring it was just grief that kept Ken away during the holidays.

Of course his cousin would have been thinking about them, putting their happiness first, even when he'd been dealing with his trauma.

"But you invited Tamara this year."

Ken nodded. "I figured it's time to work through some of that stuff. Christmas sucks. Not just because of my parents, but also because I've got a lot of patients who went through rough times during the holidays. Abuse, that kind of thing. It usually means I have to work through a lot of things with them, and it gets rough over the years. Inviting Tamara over was supposed to make it easier."

"And? Is it working?"

Ken stirred the milk, thoughtful for a moment. "Yeah, it is."

Tamara

Apparently, Master Ken had an array of board games hidden in his cabinets. His nieces were busy pulling the lot of them out onto the living room floor, looking through the boxes to decide on a game. Felicia and she watched them with equal amusement.

"Your daughters are adorable," Tamara offered, meaning every word.

Felicia laughed. "They are something else. I swear, all the sugar from the Christmas cookies has turned them even crazier than usual."

"Well, it's Christmas." Saying it made her feel slightly melancholy, which was odd given the perfect morning she'd shared with her doms.

"Yes, it is, isn't it?" Felicia said. "I'm surprised Ken put up a tree.

Tamara could feel heat rising to her face, so she twisted away from Felicia to keep watching the girls who'd apparently settled on a game of *Hungry Hungry Hippo*.

"We picked the tree up yesterday. I thought Johnathan and Ken mentioned we went to one of your fields?"

"Huh? No, they didn't."

Well, that was awkward. Luckily, the other woman looked confused, rather than upset. "I hope it was okay?"

"Oh, yeah, it's fine. It's just that Ken doesn't usually decorate for Christmas."

There was no way she was going to admit to the reason Ken had agreed to bring the tree home, so she decided a little white lie on Christmas was probably acceptable under the circumstances. "I think he just wanted to do me a favor. I really adore Christmas and the thought of not having a tree made me sad."

"I don't mean to be rude," Felicia said, and the way she looked made Tamara believe that she truly meant it. "I'm just surprised that he has anyone over on Christmas. He hasn't in the past years. Well, really, since he moved out, as far as I know. So hearing that he was having Johnathan over was already surprising, but meeting you here makes me wonder how serious things are between you guys."

It was a very prodding question, and Tamara would have laughed at the embarrassed expression that now showed on Felicia's face, if she didn't try so hard to come up with a reply.

Garrett coughed from his spot on the couch where he'd been sitting, silently observing his daughters.

Yup, this had turned into an interrogation, even if Felicia was obviously a bit uncomfortable with her own directness.

"God, I'm sorry. That is rude to ask, isn't it?"

Now, she couldn't help but laugh. "Don't worry about it. But honestly, I'm not sure how to answer it. I'm more of a friend than a girlfriend."

Felicia nodded, looking entirely unconvinced, but luckily the conversation was cut short when the girls called them to join in on the game that was now set up on the table.

It was really fun to play. For a couple of hours, they sat in the living room and worked their way through a variety of board games. Ken and Johnathan having joined them with steaming mugs of hot chocolate, joining in on the games. Both men seemed unable to say no to anything their nieces wanted. After a while, Ken even produced the girls' Christmas presents from upstairs, much to their delight.

It was a wonderful family Christmas, but it came with a realization that was hard to ignore.

The Christmas present she had given herself hadn't turned out the way she'd hoped.

It wasn't the kink part, either, because that had been amazing so far. But instead of just sex and orgasms, she was finally getting something for Christmas she had missed out on in a long, long time, and it was hard to figure out how she felt about it.

This was a genuine family Christmas. Family members getting together, exchanging gifts, playing games, eating cookies, having fun and connecting. But it wasn't her family. She was the girl two of them had won at an auction to do kinky stuff with.

She wasn't a girlfriend, or even an actual friend.

The thing that weighed on her the most was that even while she was an outsider, this could never compare to her own Christmas tradition. Sitting at home alone, watching Christmas movies simply held no appeal when this was the alternative. Being here was so much better.

This was something that she'd unknowingly longed for all these years. She'd made up for it in the best way she could, but just maybe it was time to start thinking about looking for a family of her own. Looking for something serious. A relationship that might lead to more, rather than a short-time arrangement.

Maybe her plan had backfired. She had wanted to treat herself to something wild and break out of the pattern of playing things safe, not moving forward in her life. Instead, she felt her eyes move between Master Johnathan and Master Ken.

Plans changed.

Chapter Fourteen

December 25th

Ken

He needed a break. He adored his nieces and Felicia. And Garret was a good guy, too, but it was getting too much and he was self-aware enough to admit that to himself. After years of pulling away from his family during the holidays, seeing them happy and relaxed at his place was a pretty stark punch of reality.

He'd missed out on seeing this every single year.

"I'm going to head out for a walk." Grabbing his coat in the hallway, he noticed Tamara had followed him.

"Do you want company?" Even though she was waiting for his answer, he could tell from her expression that she already knew the answer.

"No, thank you. Not right now. But thank you for the offer, darling." She really had been sweet, the way she'd gone with the turn of events, playing with Mellie and Cora, never looking like the unexpected interruption of their plans was bothering her. And all that despite his hyper nieces and nosy cousin.

Tamara nodded. "Of course."

She accepted that he wasn't in the mood for company, and that without feeling rejected. It was another thing he appreciated about her.

Heading outside, he felt the icy cold air blow against his skin and quickly pulled a hat and mittens from his coat pockets. He hadn't grabbed a scarf, and immediately regretted it, but he wasn't about to go back in. Instead, he headed down the street, getting some much-needed distance to clear his head.

When he'd planned on taking a step towards improving his mental attitude over the holidays, he hadn't planned on being thrown into the deep water, and as much as he'd enjoyed everyone's company, he was reaching the limit of his comfort zone.

Time to re-group and take a step back.

Tamara

The door closed in front of her. Starting at it for a couple of seconds, she shook herself. Turning, she headed back into the living room where Felicia was maneuvering her girls skillfully toward the hallway, instructing them to put on their shoes. Within five minutes—a record speed if anyone asked Tamara—, Felicia and Garret had said their goodbyes and gotten their somewhat reluctant daughters out of the door.

Clearly, they had interpreted Master Ken's decision to go for a walk as a sign that he needed some space.

In the living room, Johnathan was picking up the last of the wrapping paper. Bending down, she added to the garbage bin he'd pulled to the middle of the room. Somehow, the girls had managed to shred the paper completely. It was almost impressive.

"Your nieces are lovely."

Master Johnathan smiled. "Yeah, they're all right."

"You love them."

He nodded in response. "It's hard not to, even though my sister really doesn't know when to give someone a break."

"Yeah." She looked at the hallway. "Looks like he needed some time to himself."

Master Johnathan didn't comment, and she decided not to pry into his thoughts. After all, it was the day Master Ken's parents had died, no matter how many years ago. Giving him some space seemed the least she could do.

She picked up the garbage and emptied it into the larger one in the utility room before heading back to join Master Johnathan. Looked like it was just them for now.

"Come on," he said, opening his arms in an invitation to snuggle into his lap.

It was the first time today they got physical. All morning they had talked, and then Felicia and the kids had ensured there had been no physical intimacy happening. Being embraced again felt good. This might be like Christmas cookies. Once you started eating them, you couldn't stop.

She was getting addicted to the constant physical affection.

It really was a lot like a sugar rush.

But more than that, being back in Master Johnathan's arms was reassuring somehow. His arms were dispelling her melancholy. For now, she could enjoy what she had this year.

Except, as she snuggled closer, pressing her cheek against Master Johnathan's hard chest, a little voice inside of her told her that just maybe these three days didn't have to be the end. It wasn't like the Christmas cookies that suddenly vanished from the stores. Master Ken and Master Johnathan would still be here even after their auction arrangement had ended.

She couldn't be the only one with a sugar craving, right?

Tilting her head back, she offered her lips to Master Johnathan, who took them in a deep kiss that brought tingles up her spine and heated her body. Much better than hot chocolate.

When his hands slid up her side and cupped her breast, his thumb teasing her nipple through the shirt, she moaned into his mouth. In response, he deepened the kiss by using his tongue to stroke against her lips.

"I've been wanting to do that all day." He pulled back, looking at her with hunger in his eyes. His hands moved upward from her breast, wrapping around the back of her neck before pulling her closer for another kiss.

She wasn't sure how long they were sitting there like that, making out like teenagers, but she loved every second. Feeling his arousal under her ass pressing against her was the best kind of tease. It stoked her own passion, and she wiggled a little, teasing him into taking things further, which he did by sliding his other hand under her shirt, finally touching her breasts with no barriers between them.

"I better take advantage of these while I can." His chuckle was low and laced with growing arousal. Like he had developed a taste for Christmas cookies.

"There is no reason we can't continue doing this after tomorrow." She didn't really think through the words, not clarifying what she meant. Really, her words could mean anything from occasionally scening at the club, to random hook-ups, to what she really meant. That perhaps they might go out on some dates and see if this could be more.

She liked both him and Ken and they definitely clicked on the kink level, so why not give things a shot? It had been a long time since she'd put herself out there like this, but these two men seemed worth it. Johnathan, with his cheeky charm, brought out her own optimism and positive nature, and she loved the insightfulness and honest consideration Ken brought to every conversation. Maybe it was greedy to want to keep both of them in her life, but the words were out now. Nothing to do but wait for Johnathan's response.

Except Johnathan pulled back, his hand sinking down. Out of her shirt.

"I don't think I'm the right person," he said, hesitantly.

The disappointment that rushed through her equaled pain, which was ridiculous since she really hardly knew him. It wasn't like she was in love with the guy. She just liked him and thought it would have been nice to see each other beyond this three-day stint.

But he clearly didn't.

Trying to keep her expression neutral, she tried to decide how long she needed to keep eye contact before she could look away without seeming like he'd hurt her. She doubted it was the sex that was lacking for him. He'd seemed to enjoy himself just fine so far, so it must be her personality that he didn't find appealing.

Finally breaking eye contact, a more reasonable voice asserted that maybe he simply wasn't interested in dating.

Whatever the case, things had gone from lava level sexy to awkward really quick.

"Right, that's fine, of course." Sitting up, she straightened her back. "I think I'll head upstairs to take a bath. I'm sure Ken will be back soon."

Johnathan didn't disagree, so she did the cowardly thing and fled upstairs, back to the familiar company off her tiny tree.

Johnathan

He was feeling fucking guilty. He'd hurt Tamara. That much was obvious, but when she'd asked him if he wanted to get together after this auction stint, he hadn't been able to think of a better way to let her down easy.

He saw how good she was for Ken, and it would have been an ass move to get in the way of that. Plus, if things came down to it, his cousin definitely had dibs on her. Still, he hadn't meant to hurt her feelings. Especially because if it was any other way, he would have jumped at the opportunity to explore how things between them might work out.

Now she was upstairs by herself and he was sitting in the living room, feeling like a dick.

When the door opened and Ken walked back in, Johnathan forced himself to get up. "How are you doing, man?" It was probably a stupid way to ask, but he still did it because he wanted to make sure Ken knew he could talk to him if he needed. Eloquence took second seat to checking-in.

The psychologist gave him a rueful grin. "Thanks. I'm good, just needed some air."

"All right." It was a fair enough answer, and for today, he'd pushed his cousin enough. It was time to back off and give him the space he needed.

Maybe if he backed off a little, that would also help push Ken in the right direction. "Tamara is upstairs taking a bath. I think I'm going to head home for the night. I'll be back tomorrow, though."

Ken's brows pulled together. "Why? We haven't even had a chance to play today."

Of course, Ken had to be so damn direct with his question. Not that his cousin looked particularly disappointed. He probably was too much in his head to actually be in the mood for any kinky stuff today.

"I'm just going to give you two some space." Honesty was usually the best policy. "I'm also going to pick up all the stuff I'm going to need for Grandma's Christmas party tomorrow."

When Ken stayed silent, Johnathan gave him a pointed look. "Looks like you're going to have to show up this year. Felicia won't keep quiet about visiting today, so mom and grandma won't put up with your usual excuse."

"Yeah, I figured the same thing, but we can pick up the stuff you need tomorrow."

Not letting this go easy, was he?

"Might as well get a good night's sleep in my own four walls." He purposefully grinned at his cousin, hoping he was hiding his discomfort. It wasn't the time to have a heart to heart with Ken right now. Right now, he needed to get some air himself, and the easiest way to do that was to head to his own place for the night.

Him being gone for the night might give Ken and Tamara time to themselves and hopefully Tamara could work her magic and convince Ken to take the chance Johnathan had just thrown back in her face.

At least that would mean a merry Christmas for Ken for once.

Chapter Fifteen

December 25th

Ken

Well, damn. Grabbing the bottle of Macallan, he watched the amber liquid fall into the glass.

Why was it always easier working with patients than dealing with his own stuff?

Clearly, he hadn't succeeded tonight. His plan had been to have a few days of a good time to bridge over the few days of the year that he usually found hard to handle. And just maybe make a new connection with someone he'd figured might be a good match for him. Instead, he'd done the very thing he'd tried to avoid since moving out on his own more than a decade ago.

Offend his caring family with his sour mood.

He'd obviously scared everyone off with his abrupt departure. He'd ended up being gone longer than he'd intended. Reflecting on yesterday and today, he was relieved he hadn't dwelt on negative thoughts like he had in the past. When he'd returned, Felicia, Garret, and the girls had already left, and Johnathan had been quick to follow. Only Tamara, who was bound by a deal that benefited a charity, hadn't run off.

The thing he couldn't figure out was what Johnathan meant when he'd said he wanted to give him and Tamara some time. Wasn't that exactly what they'd been doing before Felicia showed up? Spending time with Tamara?

She was upstairs in the bathroom now, taking a bath. On the surface, it was a clear sign she wanted some time to herself. Then again, she might just be trying to give him space.

Only one way to find out.

Climbing the stairs with his glass in hand, he paused at the closed door. Deciding this wasn't a time to assert his dominance, he knocked.

"I'm home. Want some company?"

There was a moment of pause before Tamara's voice came out, sounding somewhat guilty. "I wouldn't mind being alone for a little while, if that's okay?"

Something was going on. If his dom senses had an alarm, it would be ringing right this moment. Jingle bells, probably, just to make matters worse. "Of course, you can have your time. That's no problem. I'll be downstairs if you'd like to join me after. Otherwise, have a good night."

Perhaps on a different day he would have pushed more, but he wasn't feeling centered enough to get into a proper headspace at the moment, so this was the better way to go. At least for tonight.

"Okay. Good night, Ken. Thank you." She was awfully polite. And something about that bothered him immensely.

Time to revisit his game plan.

December 26th

Johnathan

Apparently, it took a hot cup of coffee in the morning to clue him in that he'd messed up. Or maybe he'd known it before, but hadn't wanted to admit it. It didn't matter.

Had Ken been pushing him and his family away because he was trying to be some sort of hero, protecting them from his bad moods? That stuff was bullshit.

Tapping his fingers on the counter of his rental apartment, he took another sip. He didn't need to live in this place, and staying with Ken for just a couple of days had made him reconsider his choice of going with the bare minimum of living arrangements. He'd been focused on saving money, knowing one day he'd want to settle down.

Have a family. A home. Kids.

Perhaps it was time to no longer think of those things as something in the far off future.

But first, he had to make sure the family he already had was doing well. After all, family was supposed to be there for you. But when it came to Ken, they had obviously messed up. They'd made him feel like he was a burden.

He put his cup down.

What had he done last night? He walked away from Ken after his cousin had pulled away, reaffirming that when things got a little tense and Ken needed time to grieve, it was better to leave him alone and go away.

Well, that hadn't been his brightest moment, had it?

Also, on a scale from zero to ten, it had been a ten of bad timing.

Perhaps some of it had to do with rejecting Tamara. His mind had been preoccupied. The way the whole thing had gone down still didn't sit right with him, but if she was going to be the one who helped Ken move past his issues, he really didn't want to be in the way of that.

Damn pickle.

The ringing of the phone meant he couldn't dwell on it for much longer.

Getting up and putting his empty mug on the counter, he answered his cell.

"Morning, Johnathan." Ken's voice came through the line. "I have an idea I want to run by you before you come back. I want to make sure Tamara doesn't overhear."

"What's that?" Maybe he had overestimated the impact of taking off on Ken last night. Ken certainly seemed unperturbed now.

"I was thinking we should invite her to come to Grandma's dinner tonight."

Johnathan would have answered if he were able to think of anything to say, but it seemed his mind was pulling a blank for the time being.

Maybe two cups of coffee would have been better. Or, if he'd added some Eggnog, the sugar might have jogged his brain into gear.

Too late now.

Ken wasn't only going to go to their family's Christmas get-together, he was actually proposing to bring a woman to introduce to their mother. Despite his somewhat tactic maneuvering last night, he definitely hadn't expected that.

"What do you think?" His usually patient-until-the-end cousin prodded, apparently rather concerned with hearing his answer.

"Why?"

He really should have added that Eggnog.

"Felicia already met her, and she's going to tell mom and grams all about her, anyway. If Tamara comes as a guest, they'll be pleased about the chance to meet her first hand."

"That's true enough, but are you prepared for their assumptions?" Because that was the crux of the issue when you introduced a girl to your family. They would inevitably assume things were serious.

Ironically, he liked the idea of his mother meeting Tamara. With her open, outgoing personality and happy attitude his mother would like Tamara immediately, there was no doubt about that. And he'd already concluded that she'd be good for Ken. So why was he even asking questions now?

"Look, I know it's early for us to consider it, but I like co-topping her. She's fun and reacts beautifully to us. I know this wasn't what you had in mind, but I don't see why we shouldn't pursue things, unless you're not up for it?"

Unless he wasn't up for it?

Johnathan paced over to his couch, which was really only a couple steps away from the counter. He didn't sit down though. "Look, I'm going to say it plainly, because I don't want you to get me wrong. I know I butted in during the auction, but I saw how much you wanted to win her. That doesn't mean you can't pursue her on your own now if that's what you want."

A momentary pause on the other end. "I'd prefer to top her together. We haven't done it much, but it suits our styles, I think. And I like the threesome dynamic. So if it's up to me, we do this together."

Well, fuck it all sideways. Always those dang wrong assumptions.

Time to man up and go for what he wanted.

"Then let's do it. I like her, man. Let's see if she's up for it. But I need to tell you something first. I messed up last night."

Chapter Sixteen

December 26th

Tamara

Master Ken was different today.

They were having breakfast together, and she watched him while eating the last of the Cinnamon Crunch cereal.

"What does your work day usually look like?" Ignoring his own food, this was the eighth question he'd asked her, and she was starting to wonder if he was trying to distract her from Master Johnathan's absence.

Not that she minded. It was nice to have him show an interest in her life outside of the club, but something was definitely up.

"Well, usually we try to schedule group meetings at the schools first thing. That's when it's the children, their parents or guardians, and school reps, and sometimes nurses, who get together and chat about the child protection plans I help to develop for the families. After that I do house visits and deal with any emails and calls that come up. Really, a lot of my day depends on the families

I work with in a given week. In the afternoons, I usually end up writing all my reports."

His eyes never left her, making this feel a lot more like an interview than a casual breakfast. Not that he hadn't been attentive the previous days. But today there was a new intensity to his focus.

It felt nice, but also slightly disconcerting, something she was fairly certain doms enjoyed doing to subs. If anyone asked her when she got back to the club, she'd easily be able to confirm that Master Ken and Master Johnathan both counted as the most skilled doms she'd ever played with.

"What made you choose a career in social work?"

Yup, this was no longer breakfast chatter. She put down the spoon that she'd managed to bring half-way to her mouth after finishing her last answer.

"I was in foster care. Moved through a few different homes. It's not a bad system, but it needs people who care about the kids working in it, otherwise things easily fall through the cracks. So I figured I'd be one of those people."

Master Ken's appreciative nod warmed her, soothing some of the confusion she'd been feeling since last night.

"I went into psychology for similar reasons."

He was sharing. Given his moodiness over the past few days, she hadn't expected him to go from avoidance to sharing over night. Especially not since last night he'd seemed to retreat.

"When my parents died, my aunt and uncle took me in right away. And if they hadn't I would have gone to stay with my grandmother. She wanted to take me, too, but they all decided putting me together with Johnathan and Felicia would be the best way to go. I never even had a second where I needed to worry about what would happen to me. They picked me up, had the guest room transformed into a permanent room for me within a day, and that was that. They never viewed it as a burden either. It was what family did, and I never felt any anxiety or guilt about living with them." He paused and looked through the open kitchen door and through the living room at the Christmas tree that was standing outside on the deck.

When he looked back at her, he smiled ruefully. "Except around the holidays that is."

The mood was growing somber, and she couldn't resist stretching out her hand to place it over his, offering comfort as best she could without risking him stopping his story.

He gave her a wry smile, but kept his hand under hers, allowing her to support him as he shared. It was a win that made her smile.

"My aunt made sure I got to see psychologists to work through my grief, but it took a while to find someone I felt comfortable with and then, as I got older, I switched to someone else again. I think there are different times in our lives when we need different forms of support, offered by different people, but it was still challenging to go into new offices to people who needed me to share some of my most private thoughts in order for them to even have a hope of helping me."

When he stopped, Tamara squeezed his hand, but he didn't look upset, instead he was smiling.

"Luckily there are damn good people out there. And I decided I wanted to be like them."

"It must have worked for you? Therapy, I mean?" She held his gaze, willing him to expose even more of himself to her.

After what she'd witnessed and heard about Master Ken's behavior around the holidays over the past few days, they both knew that he hadn't worked through his issues yet. She might be submissive, but as a social worker, she also had a deeply ingrained need to help. And right now there wasn't another person in the world she wanted to be there for more than him.

Ken leaned back, crossing his arms in a universal posture of creating a barrier. It made her heart drop.

She'd pushed him too hard.

"You're a pushy one, aren't you?" The accompanying look sent a sizzling feeling through her. It was full of dominance. Still, she wasn't going to let her hormones get the better of her right now.

"It's part of my job, as I am sure it's part of yours." She gave him her widest, most inviting smile and he laughed.

"Don't worry, I'm not cutting you out. I just needed a moment to think about my answer. Being self-aware is important, but not always easy."

She nodded at that. It was part of why she loved being submissive. Being able to surrender control to someone else, someone who could help you explore your innermost desires and wishes was amazing.

Which was why she needed to rethink her play practice. The way she'd been going about things, playing with the same people but without genuine commitment had been good for a while, but if she wanted to have someone truly help her explore her emotions and needs, she'd need to surrender more control. Trust more completely.

Love, maybe.

"Therapy worked, yes. There are many things it worked for. Saying goodbye to my parents, holding on to healthy memories that don't cause me pain, creating a good family bond with my aunt, uncle, Johnathan, and

Felicia. All of those things worked really well, partly because of the psychologists I worked with as a teen. And then there are issues I am just tackling now. My dislike for Christmas, for example. It's not only that I have some unresolved anxieties around the holidays from the death of my parents and growing up feeling like people started to walk on eggshells every December, but as a psychologist it can also get hard walking that line between helping people and becoming cynical because of all the negative things you hear your patients have experienced. And I can tell you the holidays don't bring out the best in everyone."

He leaned forward again, this time cupping her hand with his. The gesture sparked a feeling of being cherished that was so new to her, it felt almost strange.

"I didn't pay enough attention and allowed things to pile up. Now that I've realized my mistake, I'll work on it."

His honesty and willingness to admit his own shortcomings made her want to hug him.

Watching her closely, he tilted his head slightly. "Come here."

Pushing his chair back, he opened his arms in invitation.

There was no way she could resist. Snuggled into his lap, his hard arms wrapped around her in a comforting embrace. Maybe she should hold back, knowing that she was going to leave his house today, but she couldn't bring herself to do it.

She would let him hold her for now.

As if it was even a choice.

She was still snuggled in Master Ken's lap when they heard the door open. Tensing, she tried to get up, but Master Ken didn't release his hold.

"No, darling, you'll stay right here."

The rustling of a winter coat was followed by footsteps, and then Master Johnathan appeared in the doorway. And as cherished as she felt in Master Ken's arms, part of her still hurt that Master Johnathan didn't want to see her after today. Not because her ego was bruised, but because she would miss his cheerful personality that made everything even more fun.

He looked good, too. His blond hair wasn't tied back today, falling down to almost his shoulders, and his red shirt stretched over his pecs. Now she knew he'd built his muscles not only through the physical aspects of being a dom, but also in the hours and hours of work he spent training dogs and exercising with his peers.

"Come here," he demanded when he stepped into the kitchen. His voice was firm, but his eyes were gentle. Knowing.

Heat rose to her cheeks, and she fought the urge to look down or hide her face against Master Ken's chest. Yesterday, she'd taken off like a hurt animal when he hadn't jumped at the opportunity to see her again. Now, not only did she have to pretend that never happened, but she also needed to ignore the knowledge that he didn't find her appealing beyond the pre-arranged auction days.

And all the while she was still drooling whenever she looked at him.

She needed to pull herself together. Was this really different from scening with guys at Club B? None of them had ever shown interest in her beyond what they did in the club. The reason Andrew had pulled her aside for a chat was that she had only played with dominants who had no interest in pursuing anything serious with her.

Why did the same thing from Johnathan suddenly bother her so much?

Johnathan leaned against the door frame, watching her. Waiting.

She looked up at Master Ken, not sure what she wanted to say, but he seemed to sense what she needed. He let go of her, allowing her to get up. Reluctantly, she stepped towards Master Johnathan. It was stupid to feel so rejected.

This was still part of the time he'd won at the auction. She just needed to keep reminding herself of that.

As she got close, he stretched both of his hands out, silently inviting her to take them.

None of his usual humor showed in his face, and she felt a pang of loss, missing the ease his presence had brought with it before.

"I hurt your feelings."

It was a statement, not a question, and her embarrassment flamed up even stronger. She wanted to pull back, but Johnathan clasped her hands, although being careful not to hurt her.

"Come." Looking over her shoulder, he nodded at his cousin before pulling her into the living room, straight to the armchair where they'd made out last night.

Pulling her onto his lap, she was once again embraced by muscular arms, except this time, she didn't snuggle in, unable to make her body let go of the tension she felt.

"I'm sorry, little one." He was stroking her upper arm as if he were petting a cat. Weirdly enough, the feeling of his gentle strokes had an undeniably soothing effect.

"It's all right. You did nothing wrong."

"Maybe, maybe not. But I hurt your feelings, and for that I am sorry."

She swallowed, but felt herself relax further. Maybe it wasn't what she wanted to hear, but the knowledge that he cared enough about her feelings to hold her and apologize helped ease the disappointment she'd felt last night.

"Thank you." It was more of a whisper, but she was proud of herself for saying it nonetheless.

Master Johnathan smiled at her. "I've come hoping to ask you for a re-do."

Confused, she met his eyes. They were now crinkling on the sides, more of his usual personality coming through, now that he'd apologized.

"You suggested we might continue to see each other after this arrangement is over. I'd like to amend my response, if you'll let me."

Her body had given in to being cradled, and with Master Johnathan's arms tightly around her, she was as securely wrapped in his embrace as she might on a different occasion be tied to a spanking bench. She had no aversion to bondage ropes, but his arms were even better. There was no resistance possible. No way to deny him her honest response.

"I'd like that."

Except something didn't feel right.

Turning her head, she looked toward the kitchen. There, in the doorway, was Master Ken, who had obviously followed them and listened in on their conversation.

She tried to move, not wanting Master Ken to feel left out, especially not after the way he'd shared with her in the morning, but Master Johnathan didn't give an inch.

"Stay put." His words washed through her, stilling her movements. He hadn't said it loudly or with particular vigor. He'd simply stated it, and her body had reacted as if it had learned to obey his voice over the past few days just as it had Master Ken's.

Master Ken walked over, kneeling in front of the armchair. With his height and her leaning back, he still managed to tower over her. His body was close enough that it pressed against her, trapping her between himself and Master Johnathan.

"Since we've gotten along so well over the past few days, Johnathan and I have talked and we think there is more to the dynamic between the three of us we'd like to explore. If you're up for it, that is."

Seeing the teasing smile on Master Ken's face was almost enough to make her miss the fact that they'd planned this. Sneaky doms.

But she couldn't be mad. Happiness was bubbling up inside her. They were offering to keep seeing her. Today wouldn't be her last day with them.

Except, that wasn't enough, was it?

Master Ken's eyebrows drew together. "What is it? Something is making you hesitate, and it's not about being with both of us. You had no reservations in that regard before, so what is it?"

"Is this an arrangement for the club?" It was the one way she could think of asking that wouldn't leave her feeling completely embarrassed if they said yes. If they wanted a casual arrangement in the club, she'd have to fight her temptation, but in the end she knew it wasn't what she wanted. Not anymore.

Master Johnathan's arms around her tightened, and Master Ken reached out to stroke her cheek. "No little one. This would be more than just scening occasionally."

"In fact," Master Johnathan chuckled, the vibration resonating through her, "Ken here thinks you should meet our family today."

Trying not to be annoyed that he was laughing while she was working through an emotional minefield of hope, she turned to look at him. "What do you mean?"

Master Ken took her chin and turned her head to face him again. "What Johnathan means is that we'd like to invite you to our grandmother's house for our family's Christmas dinner."

"Which Ken usually skips," Master Johnathan added helpfully.

It was the very thing he knew would ensure she'd agree. How could she not? If Master Ken was willing to face his demons and asked her to come with him, there was no way she'd deny him that.

And they wanted to see her. For more than casual scenes at the club.

Joy made her excitement feel like she'd explode any moment now, but she knew that in solidarity with all the other subs of Club B, she couldn't let the Masters get away with this so easily. She scowled at Master Johnathan, letting him know that she could see right through his little tactic.

Ignoring it, he let his hand travel higher, until it cupped her breast. "Can we take that as a yes?"

Feeling her body come alive, all thoughts scattered and worries receded, and then Master Ken nibbled on her ear.

Her head moved with her agreement. She'd agree to just about anything if only they kept touching her like that.

Chapter Seventeen

December 26th

Tamara

The living room table was cool under her skin, but the tied ropes around her somehow made her feel like she was receiving a warm hug. It was a weird contrast, and her fuzzy brain was working hard to make sense of things. Her doms, of course, weren't making that easy. One of them was dragging a twig from the pine tree down her lower belly, making all other thoughts disappear.

The prickly, scratching sensation of the twig as it scraped over her skin was made worse by the fact that she couldn't see. The blindfold took care of that, only the woodsy scent giving away what they were using on her.

"Look at that pretty blush," Master Ken murmured next to her head. That meant it must be Master Johnathan using the Christmas tree branch in this very unholy manner.

"She sure looks nice, all wrapped up for us, like a present."

She tried to move, but the restraint they had used over her forehead left her little room to turn. It was one of

Master Ken's silky ties and the fabric felt nice against her skin, even if it trapped her in place.

Right where she felt safe.

The sinking feeling was different this time. It wasn't her first time in subspace, but usually she got there through intense sexual arousal mixed with light pain. This time, they hadn't even touched her properly yet, avoiding her breasts and pussy completely. It was like knowing the presents were under the tree but not being allowed to open them yet. Exciting, but insanely difficult to bear at the same time.

Except the things they did do, were driving her insane. The prickly twig scraped the sensitive skin on her belly and thighs, reminding her of little bites. Master Ken's gentle fingers drew circles over her collarbones, driving her crazy each time she thought he'd dip lower and finally touch her breasts. Their murmurs as they admired her body were the perfect background music for her mind to lose touch with time. It was a level of play she hadn't explored with anyone else before. More sensual. More emotional.

They had enclosed her in their bindings, giving her support and warmth. Each restraint was a reminder that they were there to hold and protect her, not just during this scene. This felt more like a promise.

"I think she's starting to drift, cuz," Master Johnathan's voice was low. It sounded like it came from a distance, even though part of her knew he must be close.

There was no more scraping. Warm hands were sliding up and down her legs and arms. They were everywhere. Their hands traveled, exploring. Over her shoulders, hips, down her legs, over her belly. Everywhere they left trails of tingling where her skin craved the touch, begging for more. It was soothing and exciting, her brain unsure how to process it all.

Then, one hand slid up between her breasts until it wrapped, ever so gently, around her throat and the sinking feeling morphed into a falling sensation. Not bad, but dizzying. She wasn't afraid of the landing, but she lost track of where she was.

Her entire body jolted as something pressed against her clit. One moment it pressed down, and the next it vibrated. She tensed at the overwhelming feeling, and yet she needed more. Fingers pinched both her nipples at once. Too much. It hurt. But also oh so good.

A mouth landed on hers, Master Johnathan's masculine scent enveloping her. His lips were demanding, teasing. The vibrator moved, circling around her clit until Master Ken pressed it down again. Right on top.

Her core tightened, more and more, until it was almost painful.

Fingers entered her. Slick, hot. Moving.

Her nipples were being pulled, twisted. Tortured. Teased.

And then the vibrator's settings witched to something higher, and two mouths landed on her nipples.

She'd been flying, and now she was falling into the abyss. Except, instead of hitting the ground, ripples of an explosion caught her in the air and she flew everywhere at once, the ropes and hands holding her the only thing ensuring she didn't splinter but stayed whole.

Ken

After the excitement of the morning, which had spilled over into mid-day in a very satisfying way, there had been little time before they needed to head out. Stepping through the door, his aunt enveloped him in her arms. Her hug was so fierce, he had to tug back gently for her to release him.

It was good he was here.

He shouldn't have waited so long, but the joy in his aunt's eyes as she looked at him now reminded him of what he always told his patients. There is no such thing as too late, just steps forward.

"Merry Christmas."

The way her eyes flitted over to Johnathan and then to Tamara was picture perfect, making up for the weird taste that the words left on his tongue.

"May I introduce you to Tamara? She's a very dear friend of ours."

His aunt was smiling widely as she took a step towards Tamara. "It's so lovely to meet you. We are very pleased you're joining us today."

Tamara smiled back, though he could see that their argument from the drive over—whether it was a good idea to spring a last-minute guest on his family, especially on a holiday—still had her slightly worried about meeting his aunt, uncle, and grandmother.

"Thank you, that is very kind. I'm very sorry that I'm joining on such short notice."

The look she threw at Johnathan was adorable.

"Oh, don't be silly. We always have enough food for a week of leftovers. I doubt you'll be able to make much of a dent in that."

Tamara laughed and followed his aunt and Johnathan into the dining room, where Felicia, Garrett, Mellie, Cora, and his grandmother were already sitting around the two large tables that they had pushed together for the occasion.

Since the rest of his family already knew Tamara, he turned to his grandmother and uncle, who were both watching them with similar expressions of interest. If he hadn't known differently, he might have believed that they were blood related, even though his grandmother was his aunt's mother.

"Grandma," Ken said, giving her a kiss. "Darren. I want you both to meet Tamara. She's a great friend of Johnathan's and mine."

His grandmother looked at Tamara with a smile. "It's nice to meet you, Tamara."

Tamara shook her head slightly, obviously having expected a very different type of grandmother. Older, no doubt.

"It's lovely to meet you, as well. Thank you so much for allowing me to join your Christmas get-together."

"Don't be silly. If our boys bring home a nice girl, you better believe my wife and mother-in-law are all too happy." Darren joked, winking at Tamara to let her know he only meant to tease.

It took about fifteen minutes before Tamara seemed right at home with his family. Chatting with Felicia, his grandmother, and aunt and uncle, as well as joking around with Mellie and Cora, there was no trace of her earlier uncertainty about coming here. Whether it was her personality, her experience as a social worker in talking to strangers, or a mix of both, didn't really matter. Seeing her with his family felt right in a way he hadn't quite expected, even as he'd suggested they invite her.

When he'd made the suggestion, it had been about Tamara and his desire to keep her in his life. Perhaps binding her to him in one of those less tangible ways. But it had also been about getting Johnathan to ease off on the tiptoeing. They'd always shared things in their life, had even enjoyed co-topping before, and yet there had been a layer of trust missing because Johnathan hadn't trusted Ken to speak up for what he wanted and needed.

Well, now he had, and it had worked out damn well.

The added benefit was that with another new person there, less focus was on him joining. It wasn't like he was never there for family events. In fact, he was there for every single birthday and other occasion, each of which was celebrated in a pretty similar fashion with all of them gathered in his grandmother's home, eating too much food. Of course, the mere presence of the freshly cut Christmas tree in the corner, laden with presents for the girls from their grandmother and great-grandmother, meant his presence would be notable to the others.

Surprisingly, the decorations were bothering him less today. His usual sense of annoyance lessened for some reason. Maybe it was the fact that he'd already had more Christmas things this year than in previous ones—cookies, a tree, albeit sparsely decorated, and even presents. Or maybe it was the contentment he felt at knowing Tamara had agreed to continue pursuing things with Johnathan and him. Whatever the case, he'd count it as a win and share it at his next session with Gregory.

He doubted he'd love Christmas from now on, not with all the struggles he'd continue to have to address each year, but perhaps his own patients would benefit from the personal growth he was working towards.

Looked like bidding on the little subbie had worked out even better than he'd planned.

An angel was still an angel, wearing lingerie or not.

Epilogue

December 30th

Tamara

Once again, Club B looked amazing.

Instead of the Christmas decorations that had stayed up throughout December, the clubroom was now filled with twinkle lights and silver decor celebrating the end of the year.

Jessica had announced there would be a special demonstration going on as part of the New Year's Eve Countdown tonight, and Ken and Johnathan had asked her to meet them here.

It was sort of a first date since their auction days were over.

To say she was excited would be an understatement.

"You look amazing," Casey said, and Andrew nodded his agreement.

She'd picked the silver sequined dress up at a thrift store, and a few strategically tied ribbons ensured it exposed just a little more of her legs than it would have normally. It was New Year's Eve at Club B, after all.

Her make-up was heavier than normal, the thick silver eyeshadow sparkling when she moved past the twinkling lights, something she'd realized with delight while walking past the enormous mirror behind the bar.

"Thanks, I'm in the mood to celebrate."

"Is that so?" Johnathan's arms wrapped around her from behind, making her jump. He'd sneaked right up on her, knowing she wouldn't hear him in the busy club. Doms loved taking advantages of this kind of stuff.

Turning around in his arms, she tilted her head back, offering her lips up for a kiss.

"Demanding little subbie, aren't you?" he teased, though he leaned down and claimed her lips so thoroughly that it took her a moment to pull her thoughts back together after.

Turning to Andrew and Casey, Johnathan smiled. "I'll have to steal Tamara from you now. Ken is waiting for us near the stage."

Andrew nodded at Johnathan. "Take care." His tone was just a touch more serious than the occasion warranted, ensuring Johnathan would get the underlying meaning.

She smiled up at him. He really was like a big brother.

When Johnathan tugged on her hand, she turned and followed him. There was another dom waiting to kiss her, after all.

As they got closer to the dance floor, the crowd thickened. Each time there was an event at the club, Jessica turned part of the dance floor into a stage, and today it reminded Tamara of the auction. That day, she'd been equally optimistic as today, and wasn't that nice? Things had worked out so differently from what she'd expected.

So much better.

As Johnathan tugged her through the crowd of people, she spotted Ken sitting in a booth next to the buffet tables. He wore black jeans and a black dress shirt, giving him an ominous look that could very well get him a role in some Hollywood movie.

As they reached the booth, Johnathan gently pushed her onto the leather cushioned bench next to Ken, who immediately wrapped an arm around her waist, pulling her closer.

"I missed you." He stated it in that perfectly serious, calm way he had when he talked about his emotions. Honest and straightforward. It made her feel all warm and fuzzy. Especially when his lips met hers. His kiss was less demanding than Johnathan's had been, but no less intense. It, too, was filled with the promise of more.

"I think it ought to start soon," Johnathan announced from the other side of the booth. "Lift your feet in my lap, sweetheart."

She complied with his demand, finding that she had to stretch to reach him. It forced her to scoot to the very edge of her seat. Ken's arm gave her support, keeping her from sliding to the floor, while Johnathan tugged her feet into the right position to give her a massage.

With each man taking charge of part of her body, she realized they had restrained her, once again, with no toys. Except that they didn't make any further moves to touch her. Instead, they began chatting about their week and the fact that Johnathan was going to cancel the lease on his apartment.

"Wait, what did you say? You're going to move into Ken's house?"

Johnathan nodded. "Yup, I was considering buying a place in his neighborhood at first, but he convinced me to give this a try first."

When she turned to look at Ken, he grinned. "I've got a ton of space. It makes sense to share. And I kind of like having people around to share the meals with."

"It'll also make it so much easier for you." Johnathan's voice filled with laughter.

"Easier for me, how?" she asked, narrowing her eyes at him in suspicion.

"You wouldn't want to keep moving between our houses when we have sleepovers now, would you?"

The suggestion made her insights bubble with anticipation, but she managed a suitably confused expression. "Wait, I didn't know there would be sleepovers. I might have to reconsider..."

Ken tugged on her hair the same moment Johnathan slapped her feet.

She might have forgotten where they were, if it hadn't been for Jessica, who stepped onto the stage and tapped the microphone.

"Good evening, everyone. I'm thrilled to see so many of you chose to start the new year here at Club B. With the new year starting in less than half an hour, we invite all members who'd like to join us to take part in a little ritual. As we count down from ten to midnight, dominants can swat, paddle, or cane their partner for each passing second. Ten strikes to end the year, let go of anything from the past, and start fresh after midnight."

Approving murmurs sounded, and Tamara looked up at the two men she hoped would play a big role in her life in the coming year.

Both of them looked back at her with entirely different expressions. Johnathan's eyes were twinkling, obviously entertained by the opportunity to spank her, while Ken's expression was calculating, as if he was trying to figure out how to best use this scene and make the most of it.

The mix of the intentions she could read in both of their faces was intoxicating, and she couldn't believe she had not one, but two men ready to start the next year with her.

Twenty minutes later, she was rethinking how wise it was to hook up with not only two men, but two dominants. They hadn't bothered to move away from the booth. Instead, they had restrained her right there, on top of the table, this time with actual ropes.

What was it with these two and tables, anyway?

As the countdown started, they both spanked her. They didn't take turns either, instead each man claimed one side. Not only did she get double the spanking, but the way they did it also meant they didn't rotate the slaps as much as they might have otherwise done, since they each only got half her ass and upper thighs to beat on.

Why had she thought this was a good idea?

Slap.

Seven.

"You're being a good girl for us."

Slap.

Six.

"We appreciate your trust."

Slap.

Five.

"Your ass looks gorgeous this red, sweetheart."

Slap.

Four.

"Let go of any worries."

Slap.

Three.

"We'll take good care of you."

Slap.

Two.

"This is new, but we're all in."
Slap.
One.
"Happy New Year, darling."

Releasing her restraints, they turned her around, her sensitive behind pressing against the table. It hadn't been a long spanking, but they hadn't held back either, and the heat from her ass somehow did funny things to her belly. Inciting a need that seemed to have only grown since she started scening with them.

Johnathan leaned over her, his eyes shining with appreciation. Then his lips were on hers, thoroughly kissing her. As her mind went blank and her body hummed with appreciation, Ken's mouth landed on her breast, sucking lightly.

Her scream was muffled by Johnathan's lips, and she succumbed to their hands and mouths, celebrating the start of a new year with the certainty that it would be an exciting one.

Afterword

Dear Reader,

Thank you for reading *Wrapped Up In Love*!

If you have the time, please consider leaving a review online. Your reviews mean a lot and are incredibly helpful for authors.

Until next time,
C.A. Krause

C.A. KRAUSE BOOKS

Club B Series (BDSM Romance)

Tied Up in Love

Caught Up in Love

Roped Up in Love

Hung Up on Love

Dazzled by Love

Wrapped Up in Love

Club B The Complete Series Books 1-6

WRAPPED UP IN LOVE

Mafia Queens (Dark Romance)

Hers to Rule

Hers to Control

Manufactured by Amazon.ca
Bolton, ON